#12

LORD OF LAOS

BY JOHN LANSING

ZEBRA BOOKS
KENSINGTON PUBLISHING CORP.

Special Acknowledgment to Patrick E. Andrews

ZEBRA BOOKS

are published by

Kensington Publishing Corp.
475 Park Avenue South
New York, NY 10016

First printing: July 1987

Printed in the United States of America

VALLEY OF DEATH!

The small army was massed and there was nothing left to do but storm straight into the hell ahead of them.

"Black Eagles!" Falconi yelled. "Alphas! Lay down fire! Bravos! Move forward to the edge of the jungle!"

It was another all-or-nothing situation with but two widely diverse results possible:

Life or death.

Falconi took a deep breath. *"Charge!"*

Dedicated to
The Memory of
CHRIS MADSEN
A Gentleman Adventurer of the 19th Century
French Foreign Legionnaire, U.S. Cavalry Trooper, and
United States Marshal.

THE BLACK EAGLES ROLE OF HONOR
(Assigned or Attached Personnel Killed in Action)

Sgt. Barker, Toby—U.S. Marine Corps

Sgt. Barthe, Eddie—U.S. Army

Sgt. Bernstein, Jacob—U.S. Marine Corps

1st Lt. Blum, Marc—U.S. Air Force

Sgt. Boudreau, Marcel—U.S. Army

Sgt. Carter, Demond—U.S. Army

M.Sgt. Chun, Kim—South Korean Marines

S.Sgt. Dayton, Marvin—U.S. Army

Sfc. Galchaser, Jack—U.S. Army

Sgt. Hodges, Trent—U.S. Army

Mr. Hosteins, Bruno—ex-French Foreign Legion

PO2C Jackson, Fred—U.S. Navy

CPO Jenkins, Claud—U.S. Navy

Sp4 Laird, Douglas—U.S. Army

Sgt. Limo, Raymond—U.S. Army

PO3C Littleton, Michael—U.S. Navy

Lt. Martin, Buzz—U.S. Navy

PO2C Martin, Durwood—U.S. Navy

S.Sgt. Maywood, Dennis—U.S. Army

Sfc. Miskoski, Jan—U.S. Army

S.Sgt. Newcomb, Thomas—Australian Army

1st Lt. Nguyen Van Dow—South Vietnamese Army

S.Sgt. O'Quinn, Liam—U.S. Marine Corps

Sfc. Ormond, Norman—U.S. Army

Sgt. Park, Chun Ri—South Korean Marines
Sfc. Rivera, Manuel—U.S. Army
M.Sgt. Snow, John—U.S. Army
S.Sgt. Taylor, William—Australian Army
Lt. Thompson, William—U.S. Navy
S.Sgt. Tripper, Charles—U.S. Army
1st Sgt. Wakely, Richard—U.S. Army
S.Sgt. Whitaker, George—Australian Army
Gunnery Sgt. White, Jackson—U.S. Marine Corps

ROSTER OF THE BLACK EAGLES
(Operation Lord of Laos)

COMMAND ELEMENT
Lt. Col. Robert Falconi
U.S. Army
Commanding Officer
(12th Black Eagle Mission)
CPO Leland Brewster
U.S. Navy
Communications Chief
(3rd Black Eagle Mission)
Sgt. Archie Dobbs
U.S. Army
Detachment Scout
(10th Black Eagle Mission)

FIRE TEAM ALPHA
Lt. Chris Hawkins
U.S. Navy
Team Leader/Exec Officer
(3rd Black Eagle Mission)
S.Sgt. Paulo Garcia
U.S. Marine Corps
Auto Rifleman/Intelligence
(2nd Black Eagle Mission)
S.Sgt. Enrique Valverde
U.S. Army

Grenadier/Supply
(3rd Black Eagle Mission)
Sgt. Frank Matsamura
U.S. Army
Rifleman
(1st Black Eagle Mission)

FIRE TEAM BRAVO
M.Sgt. Ray Swift Elk
U.S. Army
Team Leader/Operations
(10th Black Eagle Mission)
PO3C. Blue Richards
U.S. Navy
Auto Rifleman
(5th Black Eagle Mission)
Sgt. Dwayne Simpson
U.S. Army
Grenadier
(1st Black Eagle Mission)
PO3C. Richard Robichaux
U.S. Navy
Rifleman/Medic
(1st Black Eagle Mission)

ADMINISTRATIVE LEAVE
Sfc. Calvin Culpepper
U.S. Army
(10 Black Eagle Missions)
Sfc. Malcomb McCorckel
U.S. Army
(10 Black Eagle Missions)

MEDICAL LEAVE
Sgt. Maj. Duncan Gordon
U.S. Army
(9 Black Eagle Missions)

PROLOGUE

Marcel Leroux was a dignified old French gentleman who liked working with the Americans.

As an officer in his own country's army he'd never known the luxuries and comforts that most American servicemen seemed to take for granted. He'd not enjoyed well-appointed recreational facilities while serving on the Maginot Line in 1939; and he'd certainly had no luxuries to purchase in Post Exchanges in the POW camp where the Germans kept him until his escape to join the Free French Forces in England in 1942. His luck was never particularly good, and he'd known damned few creature comforts during his thirty-five years of service before retiring with the rank of *général de brigade*. Even his crowning success in the military had not been in a victory like World War II, but in the defeat in Indochina.

It was during that latter conflict that Leroux had organized and led a select group of men known by the rather unimpressive title of G.M.I. These were the French initials for several units listed as Composite Intervention Groups. These were made up of specially selected ass-kickers and troublemakers among the officers and sergeants, who went out into the Indochinese boondocks to recruit, train, and lead native guerrillas. This activity developed into some of the dirtiest partisan activity imaginable.

The G.M.I.s were quite successful within their small sphere, but without good support and backing they were doomed to failure. After the French defeat at Dien Bien Phu and the resulting armistice that ended the war, a few escaped out of enemy-held territory to return to their garrisons. But many were left in unmarked jungle graves to be listed on the rolls of the army as *Perdu-de-la-Guerre*— Missing-In-Action.

General Leroux, after being assigned to monotonous staff duties in metropolitan France, retired from the military in the early 1960s. He moved into a rather staid life on some family property out in the country south of Paris. Here he tended a flower garden during the day and passed the evenings with his wife sipping wine in the genteel sitting room of the family estate.

The general hated such a drab, useless existence. But he was finally rescued from this boring lifestyle by the American CIA. The general was well known to several top officials of that American intelligence agency. Because of his clandestine work in Indochina, they recruited him to work for them. Although this required his return to Vietnam, he was to act in a purely advisory capacity in a top-secret program quite similar to his old G.M.I. These operations were carried out by units of the United States Army's Green Berets.

He was provided with a nice apartment in Saigon and worked at Peterson Field where the Special Operations Group had their headquarters.

One evening, after having been there for nine months, the old general had just finished work. Feeling the need for company, he was on his way to join some American friends at the Ton Son Nhut main officers' club when a young SOG captain approached him in the hall.

"I beg your pardon, general," the captain said. "I wonder if I could ask a favor of you."

"Certainement, capitaine," General Leroux said courteously.

"We have been receiving voice radio broadcasts for the past several months," the captain said. "They are obviously from the same source. The transmissions are very weak and sound like they are in the French language."

"I would be most 'appy to listen to it for you," General Leroux said in his heavy accent. Although his English was perfect, he'd never been able to master the pronunciation properly.

The captain was apologetic as he led the general to the communications room. "This is probably a waste of your time, but it's been bothering me for quite some time. It just started up again, and I rushed out here to find you."

They went to a large receiving set where a sergeant sat working the dials. The captain tapped him on the shoulder. "Put it on the speaker."

"Yes, sir."

There was a continuous crackling sound, but behind this audio disturbance a man's voice could easily be heard.

"Niche. Niche. C'est Chien. A vous. Niche. C'est Chien. A vous."

General Leroux stared incredulously at the radio. Suddenly, after the speaker repeated the call several more times, he grabbed a microphone. *"Chien. C'est Niche. Pourquoi ecorcez-vous? A vous."*

There was a hesitation, but the voice came back and the emotion in it was undeniable. The man was almost shouting in a frenzy. *"Je n'ecorce pas! Je morde!"*

The French general's hands shook, and he looked in wide-eyed wonder at the captain. The American officer was alarmed. "Jesus, sir! What's the matter!"

"That man on the radio, 'e 'as just given the proper identification of the G.M.I.—Groupement Mixte d'Intervention—as a French guerrilla leader from our war here."

"You mean the poor bastard has been out there in the

13

jungle fighting the French-Indochinese War all this time?" the captain asked amazed.

Leroux held out his hands in a gesture of wonderment. "That man, a French officer or sergeant, has been obviously serving *en combat* for at least fifteen years!"

CHAPTER 1

Archie Dobbs had gotten one of his stripes back.

The military powers-that-be had actually stripped two off his sleeves for going AWOL from the U.S. Army Hospital at Long Binh a couple of months previously. It didn't matter that he'd gone from a soft bed straight back to the hell of combat to rejoin his embattled comrades of Lieutenant Colonel Robert Falconi's Black Eagle Detachment. The commanding officer of the Medical Holding Detachment had insisted that proper discipline be maintained, and Archie's position in the army (which was rather precarious at best) dipped from the exalted rating of staff sergeant to a mediocre corporalcy.

Normally, if such a thing were to happen to a regular line infantry NCO, his commander would have swooped down on the army doctor to punch the chickenshit bastard's lights out and/or get his man's rank back. But in a clandestine outfit like the Black Eagles, a soldier has to put up with a lot of "happy horseshit"—Archie's words—because publicity from such an action would draw attention to them. This was the last thing the detachment wanted, because it would cause serious compromising, which could lead to combat casualties in the treacherous and deadly game of unconventional warfare.

The best Falconi could do for his wayward boy was to

cajole CIA field officer Chuck Fagin into putting out some persuasive words in the shadowy chain of command they worked under. The disappointing result of that effort was but a single step up in rank to buck sergeant for Archie.

However, it was still a good excuse for a beer brawl. Any rank gained, even after an underhanded deal like that, deserved to be wetted down. The gala social occasion took place in the Black Eagle bunker at Nui Dep. This was a Special Forces "B" Camp located near the Cambodian border where the Black Eagles had been banished there months before. This was the result of charges against them for conduct unbecoming human beings during previous excursions into various aspects of Southeast Asian nightlife.

The promotion party almost dissolved into a demotion party, however, when Archie got drunk and staggered out for a breath of fresh air. This led to a walk around the camp. The stroll took Archie to the garrison's headquarters where he spied the camp commander's personal jeep. This august personality was Major Rory Riley—who had gone to great trouble to swipe the vehicle from a corrupt South Vietnamese air force general. Archie jumped into the quarter-ton truck, fumbled with the ignition switch, and roared away into the night.

Maj. Rory Riley's rage at having the conveyence taken from in front of his own personal bunker soared to record-breaking heights when he discovered it lying upside down in the garrison's trash sump the next morning.

Unfortunately, when Archie staggered out of the mess, he'd stumbled through a pool of cosmoline grease that had leaked out from a ruptured can tossed there by a Special Forces light weapons leader. Archie left an oily black trail that led from the sump across the camp straight to the Black Eagles' billets. This bothersome situation came to a climax when Riley made a personal call on Lt. Col. Robert Falconi the next morning.

Riley tapped lightly on the bunker door and was admitted by Ray Swift Elk who was acting as senior noncommissioned officer during Sergeant Major Top Gordon's medical leave. Ray, as correct and proper a gentleman soldier who ever sported army green, greeted the major respectfully. "Yes, sir. What can I do for you?"

Riley smiled. "Oh, hello, Sergeant Swift Elk. I was wondering—if it ain't a lot o' trouble—if I could speak to Colonel Falconi."

Swift Elk, though suspicious of Riley's unusual solicitude, invited him to take a seat while he fetched the detachment commander from his office. Falconi, who had not known of Archie's jeep adventure, had been a bit irritated at being called away from his labors over a thrice-rejected After-Action Report on his unit's latest caper, Operation Song Cai Duel. He stepped out into the bunker's main room and lit a cigarette. "What's happening, Riley?"

Riley continued smiling. "I really hate to bother you, sir. But I'm afraid someone in your outfit has been a—" He hesitated, then feigned an expression of grief and disappointment. "—a litterbug."

Falconi frowned quizzically. "A what?"

"Oh, God, forgive me!" Riley cried in mock anguish. "But I had to say it straight out, sir!" He pointed to the floor. "See, colonel? There's a trail of cosmoline that leads across the room here to the sleeping area."

Swift Elk glanced over at Falconi. "I was wondering about that myself, sir. As soon as the guys woke up I was gonna ask who did it."

Riley shook his head. "Tsk! Tsk! Are your boys still beddy-bye, sir?"

"I gave 'em the morning off," Falconi growled. He was extremely suspicious of Riley's conduct. "You know all about this cosmoline here, don't you, Riley?"

"Yeah, Falconi!" Riley snapped throwing military protocol to the wind. "And it's gonna cost you plenty."

"First I want to find out who made the mess," Falconi said. He nudged Swift Elk. "Go in there and drag the sonofabitch out here, then we'll get down to the bottom of this thing."

"Yes, sir." Swift Elk went through the door to the sleeping quarters. He returned within a minute pulling a sleepily protesting Archie Dobbs with him.

Riley, maintaining his smile, walked over and looked down at Archie's boots. They were covered with cosmoline from the sump. "Oh, dear!" he said. "It was Archie, wasn't it?"

Swift Elk frowned. "He was lying on his mattress. The thing has got black goo all over it."

Archie, now awake, looked down at his filthy boots. "Wha' happened?"

"When you drove my jeep into the trash sump, you sonofabitch, you stepped into a puddle of cosmoline," Riley hissed.

"Your jeep?" Archie asked, assuming an innocent air.

"Yeah! My jeep!" Riley yelled. "The one you stole and rolled into the sump. You busted the rear axle, you bastard, and there ain't another to be had in this goddamned camp!"

Falconi's temper snapped and he shot a murderous glance Archie's way. "Did you take Riley's jeep?"

Archie grinned and shrugged. "Was that his?"

"You know goddamned well it was!" Riley bellowed. "I stole the goddamned thing from the fucking South Vietnamese Air Force chief of staff in Saigon. I went to all the trouble of repainting it and bullshitting its way aboard a C-130 for the flight over here." He turned on Falconi. "You owe me, you bastard! *You owe me!*"

Falconi gritted his teeth. What Riley said was absolutely true. "Okay. Okay. We'll work something out."

Swift Elk grabbed Archie again and shook him hard. "Now you've done it!"

"Aw, lemme alone!" Archie protested.

Riley calmed down and smiled. He walked over to the refrigerator sitting in the corner of the bunker. "This," he said leaning against it, "will settle the debt nicely."

Archie went pale.

Swift Elk's mouth popped open wide in shock.

Falconi yelled, "Not the fucking refrigerator, Riley!"

"Yes," Riley said. "The fucking refrigerator."

Swift Elk grabbed Archie once more. This time he shoved him up against the wall. "See what you've done, you drunken asshole!"

"But, Riley," Falconi protested. "It's the only refrigerator in Nui Dep. My Supply Sergeant Valverede promoted it himself. He worked his ass off to steal it out of an ARVN officers' club."

"The refrigerator," Riley announced, making the decision final. "I am a wronged party and I demand a rightful settlement for the destruction of my beloved jeep." He walked to the door of the bunker. "I'll have a detail of my guys over to pick it up in about fifteen minutes." He saluted in an exaggerated manner. "Good day, *sir!*" Then, laughing, he went through the blackout curtain and ascended the stairs to ground level.

Archie swallowed hard and displayed a weak grin. "I guess I had a little too much to drink last night."

There were fourteen men assigned to the Black Eagle Detachment. Ten were in good standing on active duty, two were on administrative furlough, and one was on medical leave, and one was on everybody's shit list.

That was Sgt. Archie Dobbs.

On the evening following the removal of the refrigerator, his acquaintances—he no longer had any friends—sipped their warm beer as they all sat on top of their bunker discussing the horrible turn of events that had occurred.

19

Each and every one glowered at Archie in silent rage. Even the three new guys—Matsamura, Simpson, and Robichaux—would have nothing to do with him.

Archie was so upset and ashamed of himself that he drank nothing but a little tepid water from his canteen. He'd made several sincere and heartfelt attempts to apologize and beg for forgiveness, but his sin was unpardonable. In the tropical hell of Vietnam, a man could put up with the steamy heart during the blistering afternoons as long as he knew that there was ice cold beer waiting for him at the end of the day. A shower, followed by a filling nutritious meal of C-rations augmented with some locally procured fish or pork, could not be topped off better than by gurgling frosty, belch-producing brew.

The problem wasn't helped much when a couple of Riley's wise-guy sergeants walked by. They stopped and one called out, "Who's the medic now that Malpractice McCorckel is on leave?"

"I am," Doc Robicheaux said. The navy corpsman, one of the new men who had only recently arrived, stood up. "You guys need something?"

"Yeah!" the wag cracked. "Have you got anything for a frostbitten throat? Them cold suds we been drinking all evening is having a bad effect on us." He and his buddy cackled loudly, then swaggered off toward their billets.

Archie groaned in his disgrace and hung his head even lower.

The morbid gathering continued on in silence until a runner from Riley's headquarters suddenly showed up. Blue Richards, normally a good-natured boy, jumped to his feet and pointed a threatening finger in the visitor's face. "Say somethin' about cold beer, and I'm gonna whup you like a stepchild!"

"Hey," the runner said in protest. "Get off my back, Blue. I'm here on official business. Is the Falcon in?"

Blue's anger barely subsided. "He's down in the bunker

20

with Hawkins. So what?"

"I gotta seem him," the guy said going down the steps. "That's 'so what'!" He went through the blackout curtain and found both Falconi and Chris Hawkins making the final alterations on the After-Action Report. "Howdy, sir," the runner said. "The commo sergeant sent me here to let you know that a chopper is coming in with Fagin aboard."

"At this time of day?" Falconi said, checking his watch.

"Yes, sir. Pretty unusual, huh?"

"I'll say," Chris interjected. "What's the ETA?"

"In about twenty minutes, sir," the runner said, going back to the door. He paused and turned around. "Your guys is sure in a bad mood, sir." Then he grinned. "Maybe some cold beer would cheer 'em up."

"Get the hell outta here!" Falconi yelled at the departing man. He calmed down and looked over at Chris. "What the hell have they dreamed up for us now?"

"God only knows," Chris said. "We're at full strength and have had a few weeks of rest. I'm not surprised we're being committed to something."

"There seems to be a rush about this one," Falconi said. "The way they fuck up our planning and logistics when there's plenty of time to accomplish a mission, makes me jumpy as hell about this."

Chris Hawkins put his boonie hat on. "Let's get over to the chopper pad and get the bad word."

"After you," Falconi said.

The two ascended the steps to ground level. Ray Swift Elk looked up from where he was sitting with the men. He finished off the beer he'd been enduring and joined the two officers. "Something going down?"

"Fagin's on his way in," Falconi said.

"Shit!" Swift Elk said under his breath.

Paulo Garcia, the automatic rifleman in Alpha Team, sighed aloud. "Our rest and recreation is over."

Frank Matsamura, another new man, gave him a puz-

21

zled look. "Who's this guy Fagin?"

"Our CIA liaison," Paulo explained. "When he shows up he always has an operations plan under his arm."

"In other words," Blue Richards added, "we'll be in deep shit soon."

Archie Dobbs stood up. "Want me to go with you, Falcon?" he asked hopefully.

"Stay outta my life, Archie!" Falconi snapped.

"Yes, sir," Archie said mournfully. He squatted back down.

Falconi, Chris, and Swift Elk hurried away to cross the camp. By the time they arrived at the helicopter landing area, the sound of the rapidly approaching aircraft could be faintly heard in the distance. The NCOIC, using hand-held strobe lights in the growing dusk, waited patiently for the chopper to make an appearance.

In five minutes an H34 came in, swinging lazily as the pilot lined up on the landing sergeant's signals. He settled in on a smooth, dust-kicking landing, and a husky figure leaped from the large cargo door and walked rapidly toward Falconi and company.

This was Chuck Fagin, and the expression on his face was that of a man in a hurry. He carried a canvas attache case in one hand and a small overnight bag in the other. "Hi ya, Falconi," he said, offering his hand. He nodded to the other two. "Chris, Ray, how are you guys?"

"We're curious," Chris said.

"Yeah," Falconi said. "What's with the surprise visit?"

"It's the goddamnedest thing we've run into yet," Fagin said. "Let's get over to the bunker. I've already raised Riley to provide isolation for us."

The three Black Eagles walked fast to keep up with the CIA officer as he led them back to the Black Eagle area. "This is gonna be the deepest penetration yet," he said over his shoulder. "And a chance to really kick some ass in a bad way."

22

When they reached the remainder of the detachment, Fagin made only hurried greetings. He turned and motioned to Falconi. "Get on down in the bunker. Time's wasting."

"Relax, relax," Falconi said, going down the steps.

Fagin rushed after him. "And open that refrigerator! After that hot, fucking flight I'm in the mood for a nice cold beer." He disappeared through the blackout cover.

Two seconds later, Fagin rushed to the top of the steps. His face was beet-red with rage. "Archie Dobbs!" he roared. "You stupid sonofabitch!"

CHAPTER 2

Chuck Fagin, in spite of his hurry, took a couple of minutes to grumble about the temperature of the warm beer. He forced himself to take a few more sips. "I'm really disappointed," he said in a classic understatement. "You gotta keep more control on that dumb-ass Archie."

"Tell me about it," Falconi said.

Fagin finally settled down for business. He, Falconi, Chris Hawkins, and Ray Swift Elk were seated in the colonel's small office. Falconi opened his attache case and pulled out a sheaf of mimeographed documents.

Swift Elk glanced at them. "Does that paperwork represent our next mission?"

"It sure does," Fagin said. "It's a little operation the brass have christened 'Operation Lord of Laos.' " He gave each man a similar set of the operation plan. "Like I said over at the chopper pad, guys, this is the goddamnedest thing we've run into yet."

Falconi quickly perused the papers. After he finished the sketchy reading, he shook his head in disbelief. "You mean to tell me this poor bastard has been out there in that jungle for fifteen years?"

"More than just out there," Fagin said. "He's been fighting, man, *fighting*. And the powers-that-be have chosen the exhalted Black Eagles to link up with the guy and start kicking some ass. There's no doubt that since he's survived this long, he's not only damned good, he's effective. Putting you guys in with him and his group will set up one hell of an insurgency operation."

"How soon do we go in?" Chris asked.

"We'll have you infiltrated into the OA in about forty-eight hours," Fagin said.

"You're kidding!" Falconi exclaimed.

"Hell, no!" Fagin countered. "We're moving fast on this one, Falconi. It's too good an opportunity to let slip by. The fact that the situation has been unknown this long is a goddamned shame."

Falconi accepted the decision, but he wasn't happy about it. He'd have preferred more time for preparation. "Well, shit!" the lieutenant colonel said in resignation. He motioned to Swift Elk. "Get the troops in here quick. We can't waste time. "We've got to set up isolation pronto."

"Yes, sir," Swift Elk said. The Sioux NCO quickly stood up and went outside to call in the Black Eagles.

The "isolation" that Falconi spoke of was indeed that. It was a situation in which the detachment was isolated from the outside world while they prepared for the upcoming mission. Each man would study his particular role and specialty in the operation then brief his fellow soldiers until all detachment members completely understood what was expected of them. That way, the loss of one could be made up by another who was wholly integrated into the big picture. While this paperwork was going on, there would be other staff preparations such as supply details, intelligence gathering and dissemination, and some hardheaded planning to back up the preparations.

Falconi could hear the men hurrying down the steps into the bunker. He casually lit a cigarette and winked across the table at Lt. Chris Hawkins. "What's that expression that Archie Dobbs uses all the time?" he asked the naval officer.

25

Chris smiled sardonically. *"The shit has hit the fan."*

Falconi stood up and walked into the room where the Black Eagles were gathered in anticipation. He could tell by their faces that they knew the unit was about to be committed to combat again. Falconi also knew they were physically, emotionally, and mentally prepared for the ordeal ahead. This striking courage, while basically an individualistic characteristic, was in large part a quality that Falconi imparted into his men by example. It was something he had developed throughout his life, and particularly in his own experience in soldiering.

Robert Mikhailovich Falconi had been born an army brat at Fort Meade, Maryland in the year 1934.

His father, 2nd Lt. Michael Falconi, was the son of Italian immigrants. The parents, Salvatore and Luciana Falconi, had wasted no time in instilling an appreciation of America and the opportunity offered by the nation into their youngest son, as they had in their other seven children. Mr. Falconi had even gone so far as to name his son Michael, rather than the Italian Michele. The boy had been born an American, was going to live as American, so—*per Dio e tutti i santi*—he was going to be named as an American!

Young Michael was certainly no disappointment to his parents or older brothers and sisters. He studied hard in school and excelled. He worked in the family's small shoe repair shop in New York City's Little Italy during the evenings, doing his homework late at night. When he graduated from high school, Michael was eligible for several scholarships to continue his education in college, but even with this help, it would have entailed great sacrifice on the parts of his parents. Two older brothers, both working as lawyers, could have helped out a bit, but Michael didn't want to be any more of a burden on his family than was absolutely necessary.

He knew of an alternative. The nation's service academies, West Point and Annapolis, offered free education to qualified young men. Michael, through the local ward boss, received a congressional appointment to take the examinations to attend the United States Military Academy.

He was successful in this endeavor and was appointed to the Corps of Cadets. West Point didn't give a damn about his humble origins. It didn't matter to the Academy whether his parents were poor immigrants or not. West Point also considered Cadet Michael Falconi as socially acceptable as anyone in the Corps, regardless of that fact that his father was a struggling cobbler. All that institution was concerned with was whether he, as an individual, could cut it or not. It was this measuring of a man by no other standards than his own abilities and talents, that caused the young plebe to to develop a sincere, lifelong love for the United States Army. He finished his career at the school in the upper third of his class, sporting the three chevrons and rockers of a brigade adjutant on his sleeves upon graduation.

Second Lieutenant Falconi was assigned to the Third Infantry Regiment at Fort Meade, Maryland. This unit was a ceremonial outfit that provided details for military funerals at Arlington National Cemetery, the guard for the Tomb of the Unknown Soldier, and other official functions in the Washington, D.C. area.

The young shavetail enjoyed the bachelor's life in the nation's capital, and his duties as protocol officer, though not too demanding, were interesting. He was required to be present during social occasions that were official ceremonies of state. He coordinated the affairs and saw to it that all the political bigwigs and other brass attending them had a good time. He was doing exactly those duties at such a function when he met a young Russian Jewish refugee named Miriam Ananova Silberman.

She was a pretty brunette of twenty years of age, who had the most striking eyes Michael Falconi had ever seen. He would always say, all throughout his life, that it was her eyes that captured his heart. When he met her, she was a member of the League of Jewish Refugees attending a congressional dinner. She and her father, Josef Silberman, had recently fled the Red dictator Stalin's antisemitic terrorism in the Soviet Union. Her organization had been lobbying Congress to enact legislation that would permit the American government to take action in saving European and Asian Jewry, not only from the savagery of the Communists but also from the Nazis, who had only begun their own program of intimidation and harassment of Germany's Jewish population.

When the lieutenant met the refugee beauty at the start of the evening's activities, he fell hopelessly in love. He spent that entire evening as close to her as he could possibly be, while ignoring his other duties. A couple of congressmen who arrived late had to scurry around looking for their tables without aid. Lieutenant Falconi's full attention was on Miriam. He was absolutely determined he would get better acquainted with this beautiful Russian. He begged her to dance with him at every opportunity, was solicitous about seeing to her refreshments, and engaged her in conversation, doing his best to be witty and interesting.

He was successful.

Miriam Silberman was fascinated by this tall, dark, and most handsome young officer. She was so swept off her feet that she failed to play the usual coquettish little games employed by most women. His infectious smile and happy charm completely captivated the young belle.

The next day Michael began a serious courtship, determined to win her heart and marry the girl.

Josef Silberman was a cantakerous elderly widower. He

opposed the match from the beginning. As a Talmudic scholar, he wanted his only daughter to marry a nice Jewish boy. But Miriam took pains to point out to him that this was America—a country that existed in direct opposition to any homogeneous customs. The mixing of nationalities and religions was not that unusual in this part of the world. Josef argued, stormed, forbade, and demanded— but all for naught. In the end, so he would not lose the affections of his daughter, he gave his blessing. The couple was married in a nonreligious ceremony at the Fort Meade post chapel.

A year later their only a child, a son, was born. He was named Robert Mikhailovich.

The boy spent his youth on various army posts. The only time he lived in a town or civilian neighborhood was during the years his father, by then a colonel, served overseas in the European Theater of Operations in the First Infantry Division—The Big Red One. A family joke developed out of the colonel's service in that particular outfit. Robert would ask his dad, "How come you're serving in the First Division?"

The colonel always answered, "Because I figured if I was going to be one, I might as well be a Big Red One."

It was one of those private jokes that didn't go over too well outside the house.

The boy had a happy childhood. The only problem was his dislike of school. Too many genes of ancient Hebrew warriors and Roman legionnaires had been passed down to him. Robert was a kid who liked action, adventure, and plenty of it. The only serious studying he ever did was in the karate classes he took when the family was stationed in Japan. He was accepted into one of that island nation's most prestigious martial arts academies, where he excelled while evolving into a serious and skillful *karateka*.

His use of this fighting technique caused one of the ironies in his life. In the early 1950s, his father had been posted as commandant of high school ROTC in San Diego, California. Robert, an indifferent student in that city's Hoover High School, had a run-in with some young Mexican-Americans. One of the Chicanos had never seen such devastation as what Bobby Falconi dealt out with his hands. But the Latin-American kid hung in there, took his lumps, and finally went down from several lightning-quick *shuto* chops that slapped consciousness from his enraged mind.

A dozen years later, this same young gang member, named Manuel Rivera, once again met Robert Falconi. The former was a Special Forces sergeant first class and the latter a captain in the same elite outfit. Sfc. Manuel Rivera, a Black Eagle, was killed in action during the raid on the prison camp in North Vietnam in 1964.

When Falconi graduated from high school in 1952, he immediately enlisted in the army. Although his father had wanted him to opt for West Point, the young man couldn't stand the thought of being stuck in any more classrooms. In fact, he didn't even want to be an officer. During his early days on army posts he had developed several friendships among career noncommissioned officers. He liked the attitudes of these rough-and-tumble professional soldiers who drank, brawled, and fornicated with wild abandon during their off-duty time. The sergeants' devil-may-care attitude seemed much more attractive to young Robert than the heavy responsibilities that seemed to make commissioned officers and their lives so serious and, at times, tedious.

After basic and advanced infantry training, he was shipped straight into the middle of the Korean War, where he was assigned to the tough Second Infantry Division.

He participated in two campaigns there. These were designated by the United States Army as Third Korean Winter and Korean Summer-Fall 1953. Robert Falconi fought, roasted, and froze in those turbulent months. His combat experience ranged from holding a hill during massive attacks by crazed Chinese Communist Forces to the deadly cat-and-mouse activities of night patrols in enemy territory.

He returned Stateside with a sergeancy, the Combat Infantryman's Badge, the Purple Heart, the Silver Star, and the undeniable knowledge that he had been born and bred for just one life—that of a soldier.

His martial ambitions also had expanded. He now desired a commission, but he didn't want to sink himself into the curriculum of the United States Military Academy. His attitude toward schoolbooks remained the same—to hell with 'em!

At the end of his hitch in 1955 he reenlisted and applied for Infantry Officers Candidate School at Fort Benning, Georgia.

Falconi's time in OCS registered another success in his life. He excelled in all phases of the rigorous course. He recognized the need for brain work in the classrooms and soaked up the lessons through long hours of study, while burning the midnight oil of infantry academia in quarters. The field exercises were a piece of cake for this combat veteran, but he was surprised to find out that, even there, the instructors had plenty to teach him.

His only setback occurred during "Fuck-Your-Buddy-Week." That was a phase of the curriculum in which the candidates learned responsibility. Each man's conduct—or misconduct—was passed on to an individual designated as his buddy. If a candidate screwed up, he wasn't punished. His buddy was. Thus, for the first time in many of these young men's lives, their personal conduct could bring joy or sorrow to others. Falconi's "buddy" was late to reveille one morning, and he drew the demerit.

But this was the only black mark in an otherwise spotless six months spent at OCS. He came out number one in his class and was offered a regular army commission. The brand new 2nd lieutenant happily accepted the honor and set out to begin this new phase of his career in an army he had learned to love as much as his father did.

His graduation didn't result in an immediate assignment to an active duty unit. Falconi found himself once more in school—but these days were not filled with hours poring over books. He attended jump school and earned the silver parachutist badge; next was ranger school, where he won the coveted orange-and-black tab; then he was shipped down to Panama for jungle warfare school, where he garnered yet one more insignia and qualification.

Following that, he suffered another disappointment. Again his desire to sink himself into a regular unit was thwarted. Because he held a regular army commission rather than a reserve one, as his classmates did, Falconi was returned to Fort Benning to attend the Infantry School. The courses he took were designed to give him some thorough instruction in staff procedures. He came out on top here as well, but there was another thing that happened to him.

His intellectual side finally blossomed.

The theory of military science, rather than complete practical application, began to fascinate him. During his time in combat—and the later army schooling—he had begun to develop certain theories. With the exposure to Infantry School, he decided to do something about these ideas of his. He wrote several articles for the *Infantry Journal* about these thoughts—particularly his personal analysis of the proper conduct of jungle and mountain operations involving insurgency and counterinsurgency forces.

The army was more than a little impressed with this 1st lieutenant—(he had been promoted)—and sent him back to Panama to serve on a special committee that would develop and publish U.S. Army policy on small-unit combat in tropical conditions. He honed his skills and tactical expertise during this time.

From there he volunteered for Special Forces—The Green Berets—and was accepted. After completing the officers' course at Fort Bragg, North Carolina, Falconi was finally assigned to a real unit for the first time since his commission. This was the Fifth Special Forces Group in the growing conflict in South Vietnam.

He earned his captaincy while working closely with ARVN units. He even helped to organize village militias to protect hamlets against the Viet Cong and North Vietnamese. Gradually, his duties expanded until he organized and led several dangerous missions that involved deep penetration into territory controlled by the Communist guerrillas.

It was after a series of these operations that he was linked up with the CIA officer Clayton Andrews. As a result of their joint efforts the Black Eagles had been brought into existence, and it was here that Maj. Robert Falconi now carried on his war against the Communists.

CHAPTER 3

The paperwork battle to prepare for the briefing was causing a flurry of excitement in the Black Eagle bunker.

Portable typewriters clicked amid the whirring fans as each man studied his personal copy of the operations plan. One most important talent demanded of Black Eagles, besides parachuting, mountaineering, weaponcraft, and other soldierly skills, was the ability to type. Falconi insisted on a minimum of forty words a minute, and a test in this secretarial skill was part of the entrance examination into this exclusive fighting unit.

Hank Valverde, the supply sergeant, was doubly tasked. Not only did he have to prepare the logistic annex of the order, he had physically to get his hands on the material, ammunition, and other equipment necessary for the forecasted operation.

Chris Hawkins wasn't much better off. There was a tremendous amount of coordinating to be done between the SOG Headquarters in Saigon, the United States Air Force, and various agencies of the army so that everything would come off with clockwork precision. Nothing less than perfection could be tolerated—failure would be measured by the number of dead or wounded Black Eagles left on the field of battle.

Chuck Fagin sat in the middle of it all, unhappily

slurping down warm beer. He was there to answer the hundreds of questions that continually popped up from the men. The operations plan from which they were working was a hastily drawn-up document and there were plenty of holes in it that needed to be filled with good, reliable, and accurate information. Most of the inquiries could be easily handled by the experienced CIA field officer, but when a particularly perplexing problem popped up—such as Paulo Garcia's demand to know the exact troop strengths of NVA in the operational area—Fagin had to make encoded radio broadcasts back to Peterson Field in Saigon.

Finally, after thirty-six hours of feverish preparation broken only by occasional brief naps, the detachment was ready for the briefing to begin. Falconi, as was his usual habit, gave the guys a fifteen-minute break to leave the bunker and breathe fresh air before calling them back down to get the ball rolling on Operation Lord of Laos.

After they'd filed back into the main room and sat down in the folding chairs provided, Falconi went to the front of his command. Before he spoke he looked around at them, noting the eagerness and anticipation that showed through the fatigue in their eyes. Robert Falconi loved those guys with the fierceness of a proud father. His eyes roved from face to face, unconsciously noting each personality and the military qualifications and experience they represented.

M.Sgt. Ray Swift Elk was normally responsible for the unit's intelligence work. But since S.Maj. Top Gordon's serious wound in Operation Song Cai Duel, Swift Elk had taken over the operation sergeant chores until Top's return to the unit. A full-blooded Sioux Indian from South Dakota, he was lean and muscular. His copper-colored skin, prominent nose, and hight cheekbones gave him the appearance of the classic prairie warrior. And, indeed, he was a direct descendent of the braves who had held the United States Army at bay over a long period of years in the nineteenth century. Twelve years of service in Special

35

Forces made him particularly well qualified in his slot.

The man with the most perilous job in the detachment was Sgt. Archie Dobbs, and no other unit in the army had a man quite like him. A brawling, beer-swilling womanizer, Archie was a one-man public scandal and disaster area in garrison or in town. But out in the field, as point man and scout, he went into dangerous areas first. This was his trade: to see what—or who—was there. Reputed to be the best compass man in the United States Army, his seven years of service were fraught with stints in the stockade and dozens of "busts" to lower rank. Fond of women and booze, Archie's claim to fame—and the object of genuine respect from the other men—was that he had saved their asses on more than one occasion by guiding them safely through throngs of enemy troops behind the lines. Like the cat who always landed on his feet, Archie could be dropped into the middle of any geographic hell and find his way out. His sense of direction was flawless and had made him the Man-of-the-Hour on several Black Eagle missions during dangerous exfiltration operations when everything had gone completely and totally to hell. But his latest caper with Major Riley's jeep and the resultant loss of the refrigerator had put him on everyone's shit list. Archie Dobbs would have to do a hell of a lot to get back in right with the guys.

PO Blue Richards was a fully qualified Navy Seal. A red-haired Alabaman, with a gawky, good-natured grin common to good ol' country boys, Blue had been named after his "daddy's favorite huntin' dawg." He was an expert in demolitions either on land or underwater. Blue considered himself honored for his father to have given him that dog's name.

Marine S.Sgt. Paulo Garcia was a former tuna fisherman from San Diego. Of Portuguese descent, Garcia had joined the marines at the relatively late age of twenty-one, after deciding to look for a bit more adventure. There was always marine corps activity to see around his hometown, and he decided that that fighting group offered him exactly what he was looking for. Ten years of service and plenty of combat action in the Demilitarized Zone and Khe Sanh made him more than qualified for the Black Eagles.

The unit's supply sergeant was a truly talented and enterprising staff sergeant named Enrique "Hank" Valverde. He had been in the army for ten years. Hank had begun his career as a supply clerk, quickly finding ways to cut through army red tape to get logistical chores taken care of quickly and efficiently. He made the rank of sergeant in the very short time of only two years, finally volunteering for the Green Berets in the late 1950s. Hank Valverde found that Special Forces was the type of unit that offered him the finest opportunity to hone and practice his near-legendary supply expertise.

Although U.S. Navy Chief PO Leland Brewster had been born and bred in Iowa, he was a seagoing man at heart. The myriad tattoos covering his arms and body attested to his devotion to being a real "sailorman." The only problem Chief Brewster had was that he always found more action ashore. So he had volunteered for the Seals, in order to enjoy the best of both worlds. With a seamed, leathery face and an easy smile, this veteran of fifteen years in the navy brought diverse and long experience in communications into the Black Eagles with him. He was a natural choice to be Falconi's commo chief.

The second-in-command, with two Black Eagle missions under his belt, was Lt. Chris Hawkins who, like Chief Brewster and Blue Richards, was a navy seal. A graduate of Annapolis, he had five years of service, which included plenty of clandestine operations on the coast of North Vietnam. A tall, rangy, but muscular New Englander, he was descended from seven generations of a family devoted to the sea as ship's owners, masters, and navigators. Chris had spent his youth sailing and swimming the waters off his native Massachusetts, which made him an even more natural sailor than Brewster. His service in the Seals combined that seamanship with tough soldiering skills, making him a natural for the Black Eagles.

There were three new men in the bunker, too. Sgt. Frank Matsamura from Hawaii had been in the army for six years. His interest in the military stemmed from an uncle who had served with the famed 442nd "Go For Broke" Regimental Combat Team of World War II. This excellent fighting outfit had been manned by Japanese-Americans. Many had left the camps where the United States government had placed them and their families as untrustworthy citizens of the U.S.A. These men had not only proved their loyalty as Americans, they left a legacy of bravery that Frank Matsamura was determined to follow. He was a light weapons expert, with plenty of his own combat experience in Special Forces "A" teams in Laos since the early days of the conflict in Southeast Asia.

Sgt. Dwayne Simpson also had an inheritance from the army. A black man from Arizona, his family had served for four generations in the army, in both the segregated army of the nineteenth century and the modern integrated service. He was a qualified ranger with a solid ten years of service to back up his expertise as a heavy weapons specialist.

The final man was from the navy. Doc Robichaux was a Cajun, born and bred in Louisiana, who had a solid background, like Chris Hawkins, Chief Brewster, and Blue Richards, in the seals. He'd spent plenty of time on the river in the "Brown-Water Navy" and had also seen combat with marine infantry units. A short, swarthy young man, he had a friendly face and could play a fiddle that would make a Louisiana Saturday night dance jump till dawn.

Falconi brought his attention back to the present. "Okay, guys. Let's get into the briefing." He cleared his throat to begin the proceedings. "We have been tasked with infiltrating an operational area in the north of Laos to link up with a partisan force conducting unconventional warfare against Communist troops. The man who is currently in charge of the operation is a French army sergeant who served in Indochina as a member of his army's special forces. The poor bastard was left out there when the armistice that created North and South Vietnam out of French Indochina was signed. He never got the word, and it's to his credit that he continued the good fight, despite years of isolation. The man's name is Sgt. Lucien Farouche. We will join him to further support, supply, train, and direct his efforts to increase these activities both numerically and effectively. Master Sgt. Ray Swift Elk will cover the concept of the operation."

Swift Elk took Falconi's place. "The mission goes down tomorrow morning. First call is 0200 hours. There'll be no time to prepare your equipment in the early hours, so I'll conduct an inspection at 2000 hours this evening. Each and every swinging dick will be completely, fully, and permanently packed and ready to pick up his gear and move out. Understood?"

Dwayne Simpson raised his hand. "Will we have all our gear drawn by then?"

"Right," Swift Elk said. "Hank says he'll have everything issued by 1600 today, so there's no excuse for tardiness. Now, after first call you can chow down on whatever C's you want. Eat fast, because we'll be outside and moving to the airstrip by 0300. The aircraft will arrive at 0300 and we'll board her for an immediate takeoff."

"Aw, shit!" Archie Dobbs complained. "That means chuting up in the aircraft."

Paulo Garcia sneered. "Do us a favor and don't bother. Just unass the big iron bird without it."

Archie turned around and faced him. "You wanna take that outside, Gyrene?"

39

Paulo jumped to his feet, but Falconi charged in from the side of the room where he'd been standing. He was so pissed off his face was pale. "There's an operational briefing going on here, you two shitheads! Our lives depend on each shred of information that's going to be passed out in the next hour. You keep your petty gripes to yourselves." He spun on his heel and faced Archie. "Don't ever let me hear you refer to another member of this detachment in regard to his branch of service. We're all Black Eagles here regardless of whether we're from the army, marines, or navy."

"Yes, sir," Archie grumbled, sitting down.

"I want to talk to you two after the briefing," Swift Elk growled. "Now to continue—we'll be en route to the OA for approximately three hours. On arrival we'll make a HALO parachute infiltration. A party of Meo partisans will meet us."

"How will we know if they're the right Meo partisans?" Chief Brewster asked.

"A challenge and password will be utilized," Swift Elk explained. "The challenge will be 'Who has the pastry?' The proper answer is 'The Frenchman.' If the guy you ask says anything different, you have permission to blow his ass away."

"How long are we going to be there?" Frank Matsamura asked.

"Approximately three months," Swift Elk answered. "At least, that's what the brass estimates is the time it will take to get things organized and rolling properly. Remember, we'll be dealing with a fighting group that has been on its own for quite some time. Any further questions? No? Okay, I'll turn this over to Paulo García for the intelligence portion."

Paulo went to the front with his well-organized notes. "Okay, guys, here's the friendly situation. Some fifteen or sixteen years ago, a French army sergeant named Farouche was parachuted into northern Laos to conduct counterinsurgency operations against the Viet Minh. This was during the time the French were here in Southeast Asia, so you can see the guy has been out there for a long time. He's got to be good to survive this long, but our help and supplies should double or triple his effectivity."

"Hey, Paulo," Doc Robichaux said. "Is he fighting the Reds by himself?"

"Nope," Paulo answered. "He's got a band of Meo tribesmen with him. It's a whole village—men, women, and kids—and they must be having a hell of a time. New weaponry and plenty of ammunition will really work wonders for them."

Chris Hawkins had a question. "What's the word on enemy activity in the area?"

"That's a pretty cloudy area," Paulo admitted. "Even Fagin's contacts back at SOG couldn't present a clear picture. All indications are that there is a heavy concentration of troops that surround the area where Farouche has been operating, but we have no intelligence whatsoever regarding what they've been doing inside mission territory."

Chris lit a cigarette. "Hell, they must be doing something in there."

"That's what is surmised," Paulo said. "No doubt the NVA is sending in units to dig out Farouche and his people, but have had no luck. With us and our support, they should have less."

"Let's hope," Chris said.

"Yeah. Let's hope," Paulo said. "That ends the intelligence portion. Hank Valverde will cover logistics."

Hank went up to the front of the room. His appearance showed how hectic the previous hours had ben for him. A pencil was stuck behind his ear, supply requisitions were tucked in the big side pockets of his trousers, and he had some hastily scribbled notes stuck on a worn clipboard he held in front of him. "Okay, guys," he said wearily, "this is

41

gonna be the best-goddamned-supplied mission we've had. The last two I've been on have been nightmares of shortages and shitty equipment. The brass is so goddamned anxious that this mission comes off perfect that they haven't held back a thing. We'll be going in with M16s for the riflemen and auto riflemen. The grenadiers will also carry M16s, since they'll have no use for grenade launchers, except to instruct. M79s, mortars, M60 machine guns, and anything else in the way of weaponry will be available to us. The same with clothing, rations, medical equipment, or anything else we'll need. We can order stuff on the regular biweekly supply drops or call in unlimited resupply missions as needed. But Colonel Falconi don't want us to jump the gun on this. We ain't ordering nothing until he's had a chance to personally assess the situation with this here Frenchy we're supporting." He paused. "Whew! I been working my ass off just trying to think of everything we might want. And I still got stuff to do, so I'll let Doc Robichaux take over for the medical briefing."

Doc was as enthusiastic as Hank. "I'm not going to cover the bugs, diseases, and other cruddy stuff out there. You guys are all veterans and know about that."

Archie Dobbs laughed. "Malpractice used to always harp at us about using water purification tablets."

Blue Richards snapped, "Shut up, Archie!"

Doc ignored the interruption. "I'll be setting up a clinic for the tribesmen and their families. I also understand that under certain conditions there may be women available to you guys. As a matter of fact, it would be considered an insult not to take any broads offered to you red-hot lovers."

Blue Richards grinned. "Then I'll be the perfect guest for the perfect host."

"That's fine," Doc said. "But for Chrissake, if you show any symptoms of VD let me know so I can stamp it out right away. The situation, in a case like this, will be that there'll be none at all or the whole damned bunch of 'em will be infected. either way, I'll have enough penicillin to end any epidemics."

"What about medevac?" Swift Elk asked.

"That's the only negative aspect," Doc said. "It'll be pretty tough to get any seriously injured people out of there, but with the equipment they're providing me I can keep most casualties alive, provided they're in one piece. Okay, that's all the medical stuff. Chief Brewster will cover commo."

The chief, his rugged sailorman's face creased in a happy smile, didn't go up to the front. He stood up by his chair. "The communications is a dream, shipmates. I'll have the capability of raising SOG headquarters in Saigon, if need be. Also, we'll have the latest gear for field operations, too. Our call signs will continue as before. Falcon for the command element, Alpha for Alpha Team, and Bravo for Bravo Team. I'll have others for the partisans as needed, and will keep everyone up to date on them."

He sat down, and Falconi once again went to the front to address his men.

"Okay guys, we're really going first class for the first time since our organization," he said. "But let me warn you. This isn't being done as a reward for past good services. The brass is being generous because the mission is both damned important and—" he paused and swung his gaze to each man in the room—"because this is going to be one of the most dangerous operations we've undertaken. We're a long way from home in the middle of an enemy army. Carelessness, bad luck, or poor judgment will wipe us out even though we're well supplied. The basics of soldiering hold true here— kill or be killed. And our unit motto is still in effect—*Calcitra Clunis*; Kick Ass!"

"Right on, sir!" Dwayne Simpson yelled out. His enthusiasm was matched by a cheer from the men.

43

"Okay," Falconi said, smiling. "I'll turn you back to the top sergeant."

Swift Elk wasn't smiling. "Everyone's got things to do. And don't forget the inspection at 1600 hours. Them that don't pass will have hot scalding pee brought all over them."

There was a shuffle of chairs and a scurrying of booted feet as the men rushed to their individual tasks.

CHAPTER 4

In the scientific world, the flowers were called *Papaver somniferum*. But in less enlightened environs, people referred to them in their colloquial, yet more descriptive term, as opium poppies.

The highlands of northern Laos could boast thousands of acres of this valuable plant under cultivation. What really contributed to the flowers' worth was not its beauty. Instead, men sought the juice extracted from it during the unripened state of the plant's life cycle. This white liquid, cut from the immature capsules, was exposed to the air and dried until it turned a dark brown color. After that process it was formed into bricks, for convenience, and sold to dealers who would send it on its way to various markets.

Many of these outlets were medical. Legitimate pharmaceutical organizations used the drugs derived from the dried juice to produce painkillers such as morphine and codeine. Other, less honest and scrupulous, took the bricks and processed them into heroin to be sold to junkie victims on the streets of the world's major cities.

In a certain area of Laos, unnamed even by the people living there, several hundred acres of opium poppies were under cultivation. Higher up in the hills from these fields were processing plants that worked round the clock during the harvests to produce the bricks. It was a feverish activity at times, particularly when the man in charge drove his people with a near maniacal passion to produce more of the drug at faster and faster rates.

This man was Lucien Farouche. A short, muscular individual, with a well-trimmed black beard and dark, bushy eyebrows over eyes that seemed to burn with fever, he moved about in an agitated manner. His gait, when walking, was rapid and nervous, and he had a habit of glancing from side to side, as if expecting trouble at any moment.

On the same afternoon that the Black Eagles were conducting their briefing, Farouche stood on a hill looking down at the rolling terrain that held the soon-to-mature poppies. Hundreds of Meo tribesmen—his people—labored at cutting and collecting the juice from the flower capsules. He watched the work, satisfied with the rapid progress of the immense chore.

"Commandant! Commandant!"

Farouche turned at the sound of the voice behind him. It was the only man in the world he trusted. "Yes, Ming?"

"The radio contact has been made again, commandant," Ming said. He was even shorter than Farouche. A Meo, he moved rapidly on bandy legs, an AK47 assault rifle slung over his shoulder. "The Americans will be here by morning."

Farouche spat. "I had hoped to get supplies, not visitors."

Ming shrugged. "It was bound to happen that way. I told you myself, did I not?"

"Yes. Yes," Farouche said. He flashed a brief smile. "As usual, your counsel was wise and correct, Ming."

Ming was pleased at the compliment. "I only try to serve you well, commandant."

"Indeed you do," Farouche said. He pointed down to the field. "The work is going as planned."

"We are ahead of schedule, commandant."

"We'll have good money this growing season," Farouche said. "I only wish I had some way to bank it, or even spend it." He turned and walked back up the hill toward the summit. "Another five years, Ming, and you and I will be celebrating our riches in Paris."

"Tell me again how our lives will be in France," Ming begged him.

Farouche laughed aloud. "You never grow tired of the story, do you?"

"It is our future, commandant."

"Very well. The first thing we do, after arrangements with Swiss banks, of course, will be to fly to Paris. We will set ourselves up in the poshest hotel. We'll get drunk on the best cognac and wine while we fuck the most beautiful and expensive prostitutes available. Ah, *mon ami* Ming, it will be an orgy to rival ancient Rome. Then, after our initial revelry, we will search for a suitable luxury apartment in the city and a mansion in the country. And again we will treat ourselves to another carousal of beautiful women— blond women—" Le Farouche paused, glancing dreamily off in the distance. "*Mon Dieu!* I have not enjoyed a white woman in nearly twenty years. Ah! Blond hair, blue or green eyes, and those milky white thighs and the pink nipples on ivory breasts!"

"I cannot even imagine such a creature," Ming said.

"They exist, my friend. You shall see, believe me!" Farouche promised. He continued to spin wondrous descriptions of the sensual pleasures of Europe as they followed the path to the summit of the hill. When they arrived at their destination, the two stopped at the open gate of a heavily fortified village. A couple of young guards standing at their posts immediately snapped into the position of attention. Holding their weapons properly, they presented arms in the French style. Farouche absentmindedly returned the salute as he and Ming went through the

47

gate and entered the village.

This was a permanent habitat, and the structures here reflected it. Well constructed and heavily reinforced, the houses and other buildings were solid. Heavy trunks from fallen trees were driven into the ground to serve as corner posts, and each wall was double-thickness, with earth poured between the outer and inner shell. Nothing short of a heavy mortar or artillery round could penetrate any of them.

A fresh green covering of cut palm fronds was applied to the roofs of the structures on a daily basis. This camouflage made the area virtually invisible from the air.

The largest edifice was a pagoda-type affair with a fancy roof. This was Farouche's residence and office. A twenty-four-hour guard of trusted men was maintained at all strategic locations. Farouche was again saluted as he entered the building. Ming, as a trusted second-in-command who also served as bodyguard, had his own quarters off to the side. "I take leave of you, commandant," he said. "Although I have no blond woman, I shall pleasure myself with the trollop who now serves as my playmate."

"I have ordered my latest tart away," Farouche said. "She bores me. Perhaps I shall dally with an even younger one this time."

"I am sure your choice of a woman or girl will be exquisite," Ming said. He bowed respectfully and left his leader.

Farouche walked through the main foyer and down a long hallway to his private living space. When he entered, he stopped short.

A small Meo woman, delicately beautiful, crouched on the floor in a pleading gesture. She looked up to him, tears flowing down her cheeks from almond-shaped eyes. "Please," she moaned softly. "Please."

"*Putain merde!*" he cursed angrily. "I told you to be

48

gone when I returned, Sari."

"Don't send me away, commandant!" the girl named Sari begged, crawling across the floor to him. "I am not like the others. I love you! I love you!"

"I have grown weary of you, bitch!" he snarled.

"But, commandant, *mon amour*," she said using some of the French she knew. "I do not care if you have others. All I ask is that you let me remain here and be yours when you want me."

Farouche grabbed Sari by the hair and dragged her to the doorway. He flung the woman out into the hall. "Guard! Guard!"

A young tribesman, armed and correctly outfitted with ammo belt and harness, rushed up to him and came to attention. "Yes, commandant?"

"Take this baggage and throw her out onto the village street," Farouche bellowed. "And never, never permit her to come back in here again."

"Yes, commandant!" The guard grabbed the girl, and although allowing her to get to her feet, hurried her toward the exit.

Farouche, cursing under his breath, went to the bamboo liquor cabinet in the corner of the room. A tumbler and bottle of scotch sat there. The liquor was the result of the latest trading expedition across the border into China. He'd gotten a dozen cases of Dewar's White as a bonus for an early delivery to his dealer. Farouche poured himself a generous amount and took it all in one gulp. The taste of the whisky improved his mood, and he took a second only a bit slower.

Lucien Farouche had been born in Orléans, France in 1932. He had grown up on the streets of that city during the German occupation. It was an unsettled time of the black market, loose morals, a confused and disorganized police force, and plenty of opportunities for a growing boy to get into a lot of trouble. This environment, in which the youngster dodged both the cops and German military police patrols, had aimed him in developing a catlike quickness and a wit sharp enough to survive in even the most perilous circumstances.

After the war, with the Germans gone, the situation didn't improve too much as far as decent citizens were concerned. All of Europe still reeled under the effects of total war. Displaced persons wandered about, ex-soldiers without jobs formed unruly mobs, and there was a shortage of everything. It was a great opportunity for a streetwise kid to steal and promote, and that was what Lucien did, until he was finally caught and brought before a tired, overworked magistrate.

The judge, looking wearily down on the young prisoner, gave him a candid talk. "Look, kid. If I show you mercy and turn you loose, you'll just be back in here and end up a bother to me and the police. If I put you in jail, then you'll get out a worse case than you are now and be even more of a bother. Let's save everybody a lot of trouble. I'll make a deal. You join the army for five years and I'll see that your arrest report is torn up. That way your record stays clean and you can come back later to start a newer, happier life. Now, what do you say?"

Lucien wasn't sure if the army was that much better than jail, but he decided to risk it. "I agree, *Monsieur le juge*," he said after giving the proposition some brief thought.

The gendarme standing behind him wasted no time. "Let's go, kid," he said, grabbing the boy by the collar. Lucien was hauled out of court and dragged down to the nearest recruiting station. A happy sergeant, friendly and accommodating, not only signed Lucien up, he talked him into going into the paras. The oily-tongued recruiter spoke of adventure, extra pay, and the chance to really look handsome for the girls. Lucien, a hell of a show-off anyway, couldn't resist the idea of swaggering around in a camouflage uniform and sporting a jaunty red beret.

Unfortunately, there were two things the sergeant didn't bother to bring into their conversation. The first was that army airborne training was rougher than hell; and the second was the fact that the only openings for new men were in the colonial parachute battalions. These were the ones fighting in the steaming hell of French Indochina, where the Communists were carrying on an insurgency in the guise of an independence movement.

To Lucien's credit, he was a tough kid. After some initial trouble adjusting to military life, he took the para training in stride and came out with the coveted *brevet parachutiste* pinned over his right pocket. He didn't blanche at the thought of combat duty and went straight to war like it was a personal challenge.

The young man did quite well. He went from *soldat deuxième classe* through the ranks as *soldat prémier classe*, *caporal*, and *caporal-chef* to the rank of *sergent*. In the field, Sergeant Lucien Farouche was an excellent soldier. Unfortunately, however, while in town during brief periods of liberty, he was a ring-tailed terror. Farouche fought, fornicated, rioted, drank and behaved like a wild animal. His superiors were perplexed. If they put him in jail they lost the use of a damned good fighter, if they busted him in rank they lost an excellent combat leader, yet if they kept him around he caused untold administrative and judicial headaches.

The answer to the problem came with the organization of the G.M.I.s—the *Groupement Mixtre d'Intervention*. These units were actually one and two-man operations who were dropped into isolated areas of Southeast Asia to

51

recruit, equip, and train native volunteers in the conduct of guerrilla warfare against the Communist Viet Minh. This type of soldiering called for wild, uninhibited, individualistic bastards, and Sgt. Lucien Farouche filled the bill.

In November of 1952 he made a parachute jump into northern Laos where he began an effective program of harassing and killing Communists. Like other G.M.I.s, Farouche had little contact with his superiors. Intermittent supply drops kept him going as best he could. But he loved the life. Alone, the complete and unquestioned leader of fanatically loyal fighting men, Farouche kicked ass with a vengeance.

But his isolation was too complete.

The intrepid Frenchman knew nothing of the decision the French high command made for a showdown at Dien Bien Phu. While this battle raged, he worked on in blissful ignorance, enjoying the adventure of war and the easy availability of beautiful Meo women.

Farouche did not know it when Dien Bien Phu turned into a defeat for the French.

He did not know of the negotiations that went on between his country and the Communists, and he certainly was not cognizant of the creation of North and South Vietnam.

The other G.M.I.s were in the same boat. Some lucked out and made contact in time to be evacuated to the safety of French lines before the creation of the two Vietnams. Others continued to fight until they were defeated or killed. There was one pathetic fellow who could only transmit and not receive on his damaged radio set. He begged uselessly for help and supplies, until finally the broadcasts ceased and he was written off as having died for France.

Farouche, on the other hand, began to get suspicious after twenty-four months of being cut off. He wasn't too worried, however, because his operations had branched out in the territory that he controlled so completely. He not only was introduced to the opium trade, but he was able to make contact with the Red Chinese, who would buy the numerous harvests.

Farouche prospered in this new enterprise until the one bugaboo of all capitalistic ventures appeared to grab at his profits and limit his operation—competition. With a lack of antitrust laws in the narcotics business, the wily Frenchman was forced to provide his own protection. His guerilla group, not disbanded entirely, since many worked with him in the opium trade, again took up arms. Rivals were attacked and dispatched with the same ruthless efficiency the partisans had used in dealing with the Communist Viet Minh. But with sources for arms and ammunition sorely limited, it was only a matter of time before Farouche and his band would be wiped out. He desperately needed supplies. Finally, so frantic he would try anything, Farouche used a Chinese radio—actually a copy of a Russian R-series long range model—and began periodic broadcasts. He used the old codes from 1952 in the wild hope that somebody would pick them up and respond to them.

He spent months at the task, until finally a French voice answered him. Delirious with joy, Farouche requested an immediate supply of needed weaponry and ammunition The reply he received was something less than satisfactory. Instead of logistical missions being sent his way, the Frenchman was informed that a detachment of special American troops would be dropped in on the map coordinates he had supplied.

These interlopers, he was told, would not only supply him, they would direct and advise him on reestablishing warfare against the Communists. He and his chief of staff, Ming, sat up late one night discussing the alternatives and reached a solid conclusion. They would permit the Americans to infiltrate his land. But their life expectancy would depend on both the situation and how well they served him. Both agreed that the visitors would have to be massacred within a month or two of their arrival. Naturally, the job would take deception and lying to accomplish, but under the circumstances it would be laughably easy.

He and Ming drank a toast to the enterprise, but Farouche had one burning question he needed answered. "When," he wondered, "did the United States enter the French-Indochinese War?"

CHAPTER 5

The Black Eagles had not suddenly sprung into being. They were the brainchild of a Central Intelligence Agency case officer named Clayton Andrews. And that man snarled and kicked through knotted red tape for months before he finally received the official okay to turn his concept into a living, breathing, ass-kicking reality.

In those early days of the 1960s, "Think Tanks" of Ph.D.s at various centers of American political thought and study conducted mental wrestling matches with the question of fighting Communism in Southeast Asia. Andrews had been involved in that same program, but in more of a physical way—Andrews was in combat. And he had participated in more than just a small amount of clandestine fighting in that part of the world. This included a hell of a lot of missions that went beyond mere harassment operations in Viet Cong areas. His main job was the conduct of penetrations into North Vietnam itself. As this dangerous assignment began to cost plenty of good men their lives, Andrews had begun his battle with the stodgy military administration to set things up properly. It took diplomatic persuasion—combined with a few ferocious outbreaks of temper—before the program was eventually expanded. When that happened, Andrews was suddenly thrust into a position where he needed not simply an *excellent* combat commander, he needed the *best*. Thus had begun his extensive search for an officer to lead a special detachment to carry out certain down-and-dirty missions. After hundreds of investigations and interviews, he had settled on a Special Forces captain named Robert Falconi.

Pulling all the strings he had, Andrews had seen to it that the Green Beret officer was transferred to his own branch of SOG—the Special Operations Group—to begin work on this brand new project.

Captain Falconi had been tasked with organizing a new fighting unit to be known as the Black Eagles. This group's basic policy was to be primitive and simple: kill or be killed! Their mission was to penetrate deep into the heartland of the Communists, to disrupt, destroy, maim, and slay. The men who would belong to the Black Eagles would be volunteers from every branch of the armed forces. And that was to include all nationalities involved in the struggle against the Red invasion of South Vietnam.

Each man was to be an absolute master of his particular brand of military mayhem. He had to be an expert not only in his own nation's firearms, but also in those of other friendly and enemy countries. But the required knowledge in weaponry didn't stop at the modern ones. It also included familiarity with knives, bludgeons, garrotes, and even crossbows, should the need to deal silent death arise.

There was also a requirement for the more sophisticated and peaceful skills, too. Foreign languages, land navigation, communications, medical, and even mountaineering and scuba diving were required skills for the Black Eagles. Then, in addition, each man had to know how to type. In an outfit that had no clerks, this office skill was extremely important, because each man had to do his own paperwork. Much of this paperwork consisted of the orders that directed their highly complicated, dangerous missions. These documents had to be legible and easy to read, in order to avoid confusing, deadly errors in combat.

The Black Eagles became the enforcement arm of SOG, drawing the missions that were the most dangerous and sensitive. In essence, they were hit men, closely coordinated and completely dedicated, held together and directed by the forceful personality of their leader, Captain Robert Falconi.

After Clayton Andrews was promoted out of the job, a new CIA officer moved in. This was Chuck Fagin. An ex-paratrooper and veteran of both World War II and the Korean War, Fagin had a natural talent when it came to dreaming up nasty things to do to the unfriendlies up north. It didn't take him long to get Falconi and his boys busy.

Their first efforts had been directed against a pleasure palace in North Vietnam. This bordello par excellence was used by Communist officials during their retreat from the trials and tribulations of administering authority and regulation over their slave populations. There were no excesses, perverted tastes or unusual demands that went unsatisfied in this hidden fleshpot.

Falconi and his wrecking crew had sky-dived into the operational area in a HALO (High Altitude Low Opening) infiltration, and when the Black Eagles finished their raid on the whorehouse there was hardly a soul left alive to continue the debauchery.

Their next hell-trek into the enemy's hinterlands had been an even more dangerous assignment, with the difficulty factor multiplied by the special demands placed on them. The North Vietnamese had set up a special prison camp in which they were perfecting their skills in the torture-interrogation of downed American pilots. With the conflict escalating in Southeast Asia, they rightly predicted they would soon have more than a few Yanks in their hands. A North Korean brainwashing expert had come over from his native country to teach them the fine points of mental torment. He had learned his despicable trade during the Korean War when he had had American POWs directly under his control. His use of psychological torture, combined with just the right amount of physical torment, had broken more than one man, despite the most spirited resistance. Experts who studied his methods came to the conclusion that only a completely insane prisoner, whose craziness caused him to abandon both the sensation of pain and the instinct for survival, could have resisted the North Korean's methods.

At the time of the Black Eagles' infiltration into North Vietnam, the prisoners behind the barbed wire were few— but important. A U.S.A.F. pilot, an army Special Forces sergeant, and two high-ranking officers of the South Vietnamese forces were the unwilling tenants of the concentration camp.

Falconi and his men were ordered not only to rescue the POWs but also to bring along the prison's commandant and his North Korean tutor. Falconi had pulled the job off, fighting his way south through the North Vietnamese army and air force to a bloody showdown on the Song Bo River. The situation had deteriorated to the point that the Black Eagles' magazines had their last few rounds in them as they waited for the NVA's final charge.

The next operation had taken them to Laos, where they were pitted against the fanatical savages of the Pathet Lao. And if that wasn't bad enough, their method of entrance into the operational area had been bizarre and dangerous. This type of transport into battle hadn't been used in active combat in more than twenty years. It had even been labeled obsolete by the military experts. But that hadn't deterred the Black Eagles.

They had used a glider to make a silent flight to a secret landing zone. The operations plan called for their extraction through a glider-recovery apparatus that not only hadn't been tested in combat, it had never been given sufficient trial under rehearsed, safe conditions.

After a hairy ride in the flimsy craft, they had hit the ground to carry out a mission designed to destroy the construction site of a Soviet nuclear plant the Reds wanted to install in the area. Everything had gone wrong from the start, and the Black Eagles had fought against a horde of insane zealots until their extraction to safety. This had been completely dependent on the illegal and unauthorized efforts of a dedicated U.S.A.F. pilot—the same one they had rescued from the North Vietnam prison camp. The air force colonel was determined to help the same men who had saved him, but often even the deadliest determination isn't enough.

This hairy episode had been followed by two occurrences: The first was Capt. Robert Falconi's promotion to major, and the second was a mission that had been doubly dangerous because of the impossibility of making firm operational plans. Unknown Caucasian personnel, posing as U.S. troops, had been committing atrocities against Vietnamese peasants. The situation had gotten far enough out of control that the effectiveness of American efforts in the area had been badly damaged. Once again Falconi and the Black Eagles had been called upon to sort things out. They had gone in on a dark beach from a submarine and had begun a deadly reconnaissance, until they finally made contact with their quarry. These enemy agents, wearing U.S. army uniforms, had been dedicated East German Communists prepared to fight to the death for their cause. The Black Eagles admired such unselfish dedication to the extent that they had given the Reds the opportunity to accomplish that end—to give their lives for Communism. But this hadn't been successfully concluded without the situation's deteriorating to the point where the Black Eagles had had to endure human-wave assaults from a North Vietnamese army battalion led by an infuriated general. This officer had been humiliated by Falconi on the Song Bo River several months previous. The mission had ended in another Black Eagle victory—but not before five more men had died.

Brought back to Saigon at last, the seven survivors of the previous operations had cleaned their weapons, drawn fresh, clean uniforms, and prepared for a long-awaited period of R&R.

It was not to be.

Chuck Fagin's instincts and the organization of agents had ferreted out information that showed a high-ranking intelligence officer of the South Vietnamese army had been leaking information on the Black Eagles to his superiors up in the Communist north. It would have been easy enough to arrest this double agent, but an entire enemy espionage net had been involved. So Falconi and his Black Eagles had had to come in from the boondocks and fight the good fight against these spies and assassins in the back streets and alleys of Saigon itself.

When Saigon had been relatively cleaned up, the Black Eagles had drawn a mission that involved going out on the Ho Chi Minh trail, on which the North Vietnamese sent supplies, weapons, and munitions south to be used by the Viet Cong and elements of the North Vietnamese army. The enemy had been enjoying great success, despite repeated aerial attacks by the U.S. and South Vietnamese air forces. The high command had decided that only a sustained campaign conducted on the ground would put a crimp in the Reds' operation.

Naturally, they had chosen the Black Eagles for the dirty job.

Falconi and his men had then waged partisan warfare in its most primitive and violent fashion, with raids, ambushes, and other forms of jungle fighting. The order of the day had been "kill or be killed" as the monsoon forest thundered with reports of numerous types of modern weaponry. This dangerous situation was made even more deadly by a decidedly insidious and deadly form of mine warfare that made each track and trail through the brush a potential zone of death.

When this had been wrapped up, Falconi and his troops had received an even bigger assignment. This next operation had involved working with Chinese mercenaries to secure an entire province ablaze with infiltration and invasion by the North Vietnamese army. It had even involved beautiful Andrea Thuy, a lieutenant in the South Vietnamese army who had been attached to the Black Eagles. Playing on the mercenaries' superstitions and religions, she had become a "Warrior-Sister," leading some of the blazing combat herself.

An affair of honor had followed this mission when Red agents kidnapped this lovely woman. They had taken her north—but not for long. Falconi and the others had pulled a parachute-borne attack and brought her out of the hellhole where her Communist tormentors had put her.

The ninth mission, pulled off with most of the detachment's veterans away on R&R had involved a full-blown attack by North Vietnamese regulars into the II Corps area—and all this while they had been saddled with a pushy newspaper reporter.

By that time South Vietnam had rallied quite a number of allies to her side. Besides the United States, there were South Korea, Australia, New Zealand, the Philippines, and Thailand. This situation had upset the Communist side, and they had decided to counter it by openly having various Red countries send contingents of troops to bolster the NVA (North Vietnam Army) and the Viet Cong.

This had resulted in a highly secret situation—ironically, well known by both the American and Communist sides— which developed in the borderland between Cambodia and South Vietnam. The Reds, in an effort to make their war against the Americans a truly international struggle, had begun an experimental operation involving volunteers from Algeria. These young Arab Communists, led by hard-core

Red officers, were to be tested against U.S. troops. If they proved effective, other nationals would be brought in from behind the Iron Curtain to expand the insurgency against the Americans, the South Vietnamese, and their allies.

Because of the possibility of failure, the Reds had not wanted to publicize these "volunteers" unless the experiment proved a rousing success. The American brass also had not wanted the situation publicized under any circumstances. To do so would have been to have played into the world-opinion-manipulating maneuvers of the Communists.

But the generals in Saigon had wanted the situation neutralized as quickly as possible. Falconi and the Black Eagles had moved into the jungle to take on the Algerians, who were led by fanatical Major Omar Ahmed. Ahmed, who rebelled against France in Algeria, had actually fought in the French army in Indochina as an enemy of the very people he ended up serving. Captured before the Battle of Dien Bien Phu, he had been an easy and pliable subject for the Red brainwashers and interrogators. When he returned to his native Algeria after repatriation, he was a dedicated Communist ready to take on anything the free world could throw at him.

Falconi and his men, with their communication system destroyed by deceit, had fought hard. But they had been badly outnumbered and finally forced into a situation where their backs were literally pinned against the wall of a jungle cliff. But Archie Dobbs, injured on the infiltration jump and evacuated from the mission back to the U.S. Army hospital in Long Binh, had gone AWOL in order to rejoin his buddies in combat. And he had not only successfully returned. He had arrived in a helicopter gunship that threw in the fire support necessary to turn the situation around.

The Communist experiment had been swept away in the volleys of aerial fire and the final bayonet charge of the

Black Eagles. The end result had been a promotion to lieutenant colonel for Falconi, while his senior noncoms also were given a boost up the army's career ladder. Only Archie Dobbs, who had gone AWOL from the hospital, was demoted.

During its short but bloody saga, the detachment had suffered much more than the loss of Archie's chevrons. Of the forty-four men who had either been assigned or attached to the unit, thirty-three had paid the supreme sacrifice of death on the battlefield. That added up to a casualty rate of a bit more than seventy-five percent.

After Operation Cambodian Challenge, the Black Eagles had only received the briefest of rests back at their base garrison. This return to Camp Nui Dep, with fond hopes of R&R dancing through their combat-buzzed minds, had been interrupted by the next challenge to their courage and ingenuity. This was a mission that was dubbed Operation Song Cai Duel.

Communist patrol boats had infiltrated the Song Cai River and controlled that waterway north of Dak Bla. Their activities ranged from actual raiding of river villages and military outposts to active operations involving the transportation and infiltration of Red agents. This campaign had resulted in the very disturbing fact that the Song Cai River, though in South Vietnam, was under the complete control of Ho Chi Minh's fighters. They virtually owned the waterway.

The brass's orders to Falconi had been simple: *Get the river back!*

The mission, however, had been much more complicated. Distances were long, and personnel were too few. But that had never stopped the Black Eagles before.

There were new lessons to be learned, too. River navigation, powerboating and amphibious warfare had to be added to the Black Eagles' skills in jungle fighting. Outgunned and outnumbered, Falconi and his guys had waded in over their heads. The pressure had mounted to the point where the village they were using as a base headquarters had to be evacuated, but a surprise appearance by Chuck Fagin with a couple of quad-fifty machine guns had turned the tide. The final showdown was a gunboat battle that turned the muddy waters of the Song Cai red with blood.

It had been pure hell for the men, but it was another brick laid in the wall of their brief and glorious history.

It was to the Black Eagles' credit that unit integrity and morale continued to build despite the staggering losses they had suffered. Not long after their initial inception, the detachment had decided they wanted an insignia all their own. This wasn't at all unusual for units in Vietnam. Local manufacturers, acting on decisions submitted to them by the troops involved, produced these emblems, which were worn by the outfits while "in country." These adornments were strictly nonregulation and unauthorized for display outside of Vietnam.

Falconi's men had come up with a unique beret badge manufactured as a cloth insignia. A larger version was used as a shoulder patch. The design consisted of a black eagle—naturally—with spread wings. With its beak opened in a defiant battle cry, the big bird clutched a sword in one claw and a bolt of lightning in the other. Mounted on a khaki shield that was trimmed in black, the device was an accurate portrayal of its wearers: somber and deadly.

There was one more touch of their individuality that they kept to themselves. It was a motto that not only worked as a damned good password in hairy situations, but it also described the Black Eagles' basic philosophy.

Those special words, in Latin, were:

CALCITRA CLUNIS—KICK ASS!

CHAPTER 6

Archie Dobbs completed his packing chore. He put the six bandoleers of M16 magazines on top of the clothing, rations, poncho, and poncho cover that were inserted neatly into the bottom of his rucksack. Next he carefully arranged his patrol harness—pistol belt, ammo pouches, first aid packet, canteens, grenades and suspenders—on top of all that. Satisfied he could get nothing else inside the container, he laboriously forced the flap over it and buckled everything down. The pockets of the device were tightly stuffed with extra goodies, mostly more chow and bullets, and would have weighed in at a compact sixty-five pounds if put on a scale.

His M16 was already taped and prepared for the parachute jump, and he was dressed in the camouflage fatigues he would wear on the infiltration phase of the operation. Archie sat the rucksack up on his bed, then sat the weapon and his helmet alongside it. Next he removed his shirt and turned around to face the other Black Eagles in the bunker, who were engaged in the same chore.

"Awright, you fuckers!" Archie bellowed. "Listen up!"

The murmuring conversation that had filled the small room suddenly stopped. The other Black Eagles ceased their own packing as all eyes turned toward the detachment scout. Blue Richards scratched his close-cropped head.

"What do you want, Archie?"

"What do I want? What do I want?" Archie sneered.

"Yeah, Archie," Blue said innocently. "What do you want?"

"Okay, I'll tell you," Archie said taking a deep breath. "I know you guys are pissed off at me, and I don't blame you a bit. I really fucked up when I took Riley's jeep and rolled the damned thing into the sump. And I'm sorry as hell it cost us our refrigerator."

Paulo Garcia crossed his muscular arms and looked directly into Archie's eyes. "You damned well should be!"

"I admit that," Archie said. "And we gotta clear the air on this. So I'll tell you what I'm gonna do. I'm going outside and wait for you. You bastards can come out one at a time or all at once. I don't give a damn."

Robert Falconi brushed through the poncho covering that served as a door to the room. "What the hell's going on here?" he asked.

"Something that's got to be done, sir," Archie said. "I'm tired o' these guys giving me dirty looks about losing that damned refrigerator. And I'm sick o' their snide remarks, so I've offered to duke it out with each and ever' one of 'em. If that don't satisfy 'em, then nothing will."

"Unless we got another refrigerator," Sergeant Frank Matsamura said.

"Well, you ain't getting another refrigerator!" Archie yelled. "So this is the next-best way to handle the whole damned situation."

Falconi suppressed a grin, and shook his head in a gesture of disapproval. "That could be kind of dangerous, Archie." He pointed to the other men. "There's lots of muscle in sight from where I'm standing."

"I don't give a shit," Archie said. He walked to the bunker door, pausing to turn around and look at his commander. "Them guys may whip my ass," Archie said, "but they're still gonna know they been in a helluva fight."

"Good luck," Falconi said to the detachment scout's back as he exited the room.

Archie ascended the steps to ground level and stepped out into the hot late-afternoon air. He danced around and did a little shadow boxing to warm up. After ten minutes he heard footsteps and whirled around to face his first adversary.

Blue Richards stepped out of the bunker. He stood at the entrance looking at Archie.

"You're first, huh, Blue?" Archie remarked. "Okay. Okay." He danced around some more and increased his imaginary punching. "Let's start this knuckle drill."

"Hold it, Archie," Blue drawled. "Yo're climbin' up the tree afore the dawgs got the 'coon up there." The Alabama navy man watched the scout go through his warm-up routine. "When yo're finished hoppin' around, I'd like to jaw at you, okay?"

"You want to talk?" Archie asked astounded. "Talk? *Talk?* It's the time for action, Blue. Let's have at it."

"Damn, boy!" Blue said. "Yo're as eager as a feller with ten dollars in a five-dollar whorehouse."

"Knock off the bullshit, Blue," Archie said. "The hour of decisive maneuver is upon us."

"Hey!" Blue said with an admiring tone in his voice. "Them's right fancy-soundin' words. But you listen up. The boys got to talkin' after you left and we decided it's damn silly to stay riled at you. You got us out of a lot o' tough shit on other missions, so maybe we owe you. You understand what I'm saying?"

Archie stopped his imaginary boxing match. "You mean you guys ain't mad no more?"

Blue grinned. "Aw, hell, we never was real mad, Archie. Anyhow, we're goin' on a mission in the mornin' and we're all Black Eagles come hell or high water. We want to call it quits on the whole damned thing."

"I'm glad to hear that," Archie said, an obvious tone of

67

relief in his voice. "I got to thinking out here as how I never could whip none o' you guys."

"We owe you more'n any damn ol' 'frigerator," Blue said.

"Aw, shit!" Archie said modestly.

"C'mon back in the bunker," Blue said. "We're gonna have our last premission beers."

"Too bad they're warm," Archie said, walking to the entrance.

"It don't matter," Blue said sincerely, "as long as we drink 'em all together."

Lieutenant Colonel Robert Falconi now stood in the doorway of the bunker. A slight smile played across his features. "It sounds like everything is squared away."

"Roger that, sir," Blue said, leading Archie down the steps.

Archie, displaying a wide grin, snapped a sharp salute. "Black Eagles all the way, sir! *Calcitra Clunis*, goddamnit!"

Lucien Farouche led the column of Meo tribesmen down the winding trail that took them from their fortified mountain village down to the lower valleys.

These men were among his best fighters. Although some were youngsters in their teens, they had seen plenty of action in the permanent opium war that raged through the mountains in periodic outbursts of explosive savagery.

The gear and weaponry the small force sported was all of Chinese manufacture. The arms were type 56 7.62 millimeter assault rifles, which were a copy of the Russian AK47. All web gear was typical Red Chinese issue, from cartridge belts to canteens. This equipment had been part of opium deals with the Chinese Communist buyers Farouche dealt with.

The Chicom's motive for buying the narcotics was not profit. Through contacts in the Middle East that led to the

Corsican crime syndicate in southern France, this opium went through a series of other buyers and processors who turned it into heroin to be spread through Western Europe and particularly the United States. The Red Chinese could never mount an attack by their armed forces against the U.S., but they could do their best to poison its youth using the insidious drug trafficking carried on by various criminal cartels.

The tribesmen up at the head of the column signaled a halt. Farouche got on his small Czech walkie-talkie radio and raised his second-in-command. "Ming. What's going on up there?"

"We found some tracks, commandant." Ming's voice sounded tinny and distant over the receiver. "I have sent scouts forward to investigate."

"*Bien,*" Farouche commented in agreement. He turned and signaled to his men. The Frenchman and the remainder of his force left the trail and melted into the cover of the underbrush. Twenty minutes later Ming was again on the radio. "All clear, commandant."

"Move on," Farouche ordered. "And you come back here with me, Ming. I don't want you so far forward."

"Right, commandant," Ming transmitted back. "I'm on my way."

The two joined up within a quarter of an hour. Ming walked alongside the Frenchman. "We should reach the drop zone in another two hours."

"Yes," Farouche said. He checked his watch. "That will give us more time to secure the area."

Farouche shook his head. "There is one basic tenet of airborne warfare, *mon ami*. Never spend much time on or around a drop zone. To do so will result in your being compromised nearly every time."

"That sort of fighting is new to me," Ming admitted.

"Don't forget I am a para," Farouche reminded his lieutenant.

"Excuse me, commandant," Ming said with a smile. "You *were* a para."

Farouche laughed. "Oh, no, *mon ami*. Once a military parachutist, always a military parachutist." He patted the right side of his chest. "Don't forget I still have my jump wings in the bureau drawer back in the village."

"Yes," Ming said. "And you pin them on every chance you get."

Farouche winked at him. "As I said, 'Once a para—.' "

They continued their journey in silence for the next half hour. It was hot and muggy, but not one man in the column was bothered by the weather. The men, like Ming, had been born and raised in this monsoon jungle hell and thought nothing of it. Farouche, besides being a tough bastard, had spent most of the previous twenty years of his life in Indochina, and that was nearly half of his time on God's green earth.

Ming shifted his weapon to ease the strain on his shoulder by the sling. "Have you reached a final decision on the Americans that come to visit us?"

"I have decided to kill them all," Farouche said matter-of-factly. "That is something that cannot be avoided. I doubt very much if the generals and politicos running this war would approve of a permanent plan of diverting ammunition and supplies to me to help me fulfill my dream of personal wealth." He smiled slightly. "Particularly when it involves selling narcotics to the Red Chinese to be smuggled into the West."

Ming laughed. "They are most unreasonable, commandant."

"Yes, indeed," Farouche agreed humorously. "*Sacre!* If only I had had the chance to get heroin in Orléans when I was a youngster. I could have become a millionaire without going through the hell of this damned, eternal war."

"Don't worry, commandant," Ming reminded him. "This latest caper is more than a step toward our rich life in France. It is a long leap!"

"*Mais oui!*" Farouche agreed. Then his expression sobered. "But it is also a long leap toward death for our American guests."

The deck of the C-130 rocked gently under Falconi's feet as he struggled out of the webbed seat. He motioned to Swift Elk, then pointed to the right door on the opposite side of the fuselage.

The Sioux detachment sergeant nodded and also stood up. He walked to the door and reached down to the handle, cranking it open. Then he pulled up and the portal swung up in its tracks into the overhead. Falconi did the same thing on his side of the aircraft.

The sudden gust of cold wind roared through the two openings. The sound snapped the other detachment members out of their lethargic reveries. All struggled to their feet under the weight of their gear and parachutes. The two teams, with Chief Brewster going with Alpha Fire Team and Archie Dobbs with the Bravos, lined up in stick order at their respective doors.

The air force crew chief came into the troop compartment from the cockpit. He went directly to Falconi and leaned close to his ear. "Five minutes out, sir."

"Thanks," Falconi said. He waved to catch the detachment's attention, then raised five fingers to give them the time to the jump.

The two lines of armed men settled themselves as best they could for the short wait. These were veterans—both of parachute jumps and combat—yet the apprehension was as real and undeniable to them as it would have been to a bunch of untried rookies. The big difference was that they had learned to control their normal nervousness and push away any tendencies toward panic in hairy situations, utilizing the extra push of adrenalin in their systems in

71

positive instead of negative ways. Each buried normal instincts of fear deep in his subconscious.

Except for Archie Dobbs. That crazy sonofabitch didn't give a damn one way or the other.

There were two lights by each door. They were unlit as both Falconi and Swift Elk, as stick leaders, stared at them. Suddenly one glowed red.

Falconi signaled again. This time he raised one finger. That meant one minute out from the drop zone.

The seconds dragged by, one by one, every solitary beat pounding silently in each man's psyche.

Then the green light glared.

Falconi and Swift Elk threw themselves through the door as the rest of the men pushed after them. If there had been an observer flying alongside the C-130, he would have seen eleven men, front-to-back, suddenly explode out of the fuselage to streak downward from the airplane.

They spread out a bit, assuming stable facedown positions as they fell rapidly toward the green earth below. Falconi could see the needle on the altimeter mounted to his reserve parachute spinning around, giving him a bumpy indication of his altitude.

When the time was right he reached up to the left side of his harness and grasped the rip cord handle. A straight tug and the parachute on his back deployed out of the backpack.

Then it opened with a crack, swinging him under the blossomed canopy.

Falconi quickly looked around and counted ten other opened parachutes. Then he turned his attention to the ground, pulling on the guiding toggles to set up for the near vertical run to the drop zone.

Minutes later his boots hit the thick, meter-high grass, and he went into the parachute landing fall. He quickly untangled himself from his gear and came up with his M16 ready.

72

A little brown man suddenly approached in front of him. Falconi raised his weapon. "Who has the pastry?" he challenged.

The man grinned and responded correctly. "The Frenchman."

"Hello, friend," Falconi said, lowering the muzzle.

"Hello, G.I. Joe," the small guy said. "Nice to see you."

"Nice to be here," Falconi said.

Operation Lord of Laos had officially begun.

CHAPTER 7

Farouche set the scotch and soda in front of Falconi. "I'm sorry there is no ice, colonel."

"I'm used to warm drinks," Falconi said, remembering the loss of the refrigerator back at Nui Dep.

The two men were seated across from each other at a bamboo table in the Frenchman's quarters. Farouche raised his glass. *"A la guerre."*

"To war," Falconi said, returning the toast. He took a healthy drink. "This is good stuff. Where'd you get it?"

Farouche smiled easily. "There are certain advantages and disadvantages to guerrilla warfare, colonel. Now and then we run across a high-ranking officer's liquor stock."

Falconi nodded. "You were lucky with this batch."

Farouche sat his drink down. "Let's get to work, colonel. What are your orders from Hanoi?"

"Hanoi?" Falconi asked puzzled. Then he realized the Frenchman was far behind the times. "I'd better bring you up to date."

"Yes, colonel," Farouche said. "When did you Americans join us in this war, and why hasn't it been won yet?" He gestured in a typically French manner. "I would have expected a victory of sorts after fifteen years. I should have received orders telling me where to rendezvous with French forces. Yet there are no indications of the war's end, so I

74

keep up the fight."

"And most admirably, too," Falconi said sincerely. He took a deep breath. "You'd better relax. This is going to take a bit of time, and you won't find it all pleasing."

Farouche leaned back in his chair and folded his arms. "From your tone of voice, I presume the fight is not going well for my country."

Falconi sighed. "I think it would be better to say that you're not going to like this one bit."

For a full hour, the American brought the Frenchman up to date. He told him of the no-win struggle of the French colonial army that had finally ended in the ill-fated Battle of Dien Bien Phu.

"Dien Bien Phu?" Farouche asked puzzled. "I have never heard of it."

"It was a valley in the north," Falconi explained. "The tactical decision was based on the premise that the Viet Minh could be handily whipped if they were brought out into the open and forced into a situation that required skill and logistics peculiar to conventional warfare."

Farouche nodded enthusiastically. "*Mais oui!* The little bastards can only fight if they use hit-and-run tactics." He laughed aloud. "Like me!"

"Unfortunately, they fought well," Falconi said. He finished his drink. "They even lugged their artillery up to the surrounding mountaintops to fire down on the garrison. It was a fiasco."

Farouche poured another drink for his guest. "But what of my old outfit? The paras? Did they not join the fight?"

"Of course. And the Foreign Legion, too."

Farouche leaned back in his chair. "Then my old commander Bigeard was not there, eh?"

"He was there, all right," Falconi said. "He did as well as any commander could have under those terrible circumstances. In the end, he went into captivity with his men."

"*Sacre!*" Farouche exclaimed. He treated himself to

another drink this time, draining the glass in a quick, deep swallow. "So? If there was a defeat, what are the Americans doing here?"

"An armistice was signed," Falconi explained further. "It created North Vietnam and South Vietnam."

Farouche laughed heartily. "I think I know what happened. The south was part of the free world and the north went to the Communists, *non*? Then the Reds attacked the south in their usual backstabbing fashion."

"You got it," Falconi said. "And now we Americans have moved in to help the south."

"I presume the colonial paras and the Foreign Legion returned to North Africa to engage in petty skirmishes with Arab rebels, eh?" Farouche asked.

Falconi hesitated. "They returned to fight Arab rebels, yes. Petty skirmishes? No."

Farouche glowered. "Why is it that I have the feeling you have more bad news for me?"

"I'm afraid the fight there in Algeria grew quite large," Falconi said. "Again, the paras and the legionnaires bore the brunt of the combat duties."

"Did we lose that one, too?"

"You didn't exactly lose," Falconi said. "DeGaulle called the whole thing off and handed Algeria over to the Arabs."

"With no protest from the army?" Farouche said. His eyes narrowed. "There must have been some shit kicked up, *non*?"

"There sure was," Falconi said. "There was an attempted putsch by para officers—"

Farouche laughed aloud. "With Marcel Bigeard in the vanguard, no doubt."

Falconi shook his head. "No. DeGaulle was smart enough to promote him out of Algeria. But the 1st Foreign Legion Parachute Regiment revolted. Their mutiny failed and the unit was disbanded."

"And that was the end of it?" Farouche asked.

"Oh, no. There was a secret organization that carried on terrorist activities for a while, but most rebel army officers either ended up in jail or became mercenaries."

Farouche laughed again. "Poor bastards. They should have turned things over to the sergeants, eh?" He drained his glass. "We have talked long enough here. Let's stretch our legs, *mon colonel*. I will give you a tour of this village of mine. I call it Faroucheville. I am not a modest man."

The two left the Frenchman's quarters and took a slow walk around the hamlet. Falconi was pleased to note that the place was fortified in a style that only a professional soldier could devise. There were automatic weapons in strategic locations that offered a deadly crossfire to anyone foolish enough to mount an attack against the village. Located on the mountaintop, Faroucheville was safe from any assault other than aircraft.

"You will note that I am woefully short of heavy weapons, *mon colonel*," Farouche said. "That is one reason I am glad to see you. But you brought me none."

"The situation will be corrected if things work out," Falconi said.

Farouche shrugged. "I understand. I am to be going through a test of sorts, eh?"

"You could say that," Falconi replied.

Their stroll ended back at the large hut set aside as the Black Eagles' quarters.

Swift Elk was standing outside taking turn at guard. The back door was well covered by Doc Robichaux. The Sioux Indian watched the two approach him. His M16 was slung over his shoulder and he maintained a casual air despite being alert and ready.

Farouche smiled. "I see you take no chances." He glanced through the hut and saw the other sentry. "And no one can sneak up behind you either, eh?" He looked at Falconi. "What's the matter, *mon colonel*? Don't you trust me?"

"No," Falconi replied.

Farouche laughed loudly. "A seasoned warrior, that's what you are, *mon colonel.*" He turned his eyes toward Swift Elk's dark face. "And you, comrade? What race of men claims you as a son?"

"I am a Sioux Indian," Swift Elk said.

"Ah!" Farouche said impressed. "You are the first American Indian I have ever seen." He peered closer at the NCO, noting his features. "You have a prominent nose and cheekbones, yet your eyes have an Oriental cast about them."

Swift Elk shrugged. "They say that a few thousand years ago my ancestors crossed over a natural land bridge from Asia into North America."

"Do you paint your face for *le combat?*" Farouche asked. "I have seen that in the cinema."

"I use regular G.I. camouflage," Swift Elk said. "But I apply it in the pattern passed down from my great-great-grandfather."

Falconi interjected. "That particular gentleman fought the U.S. Army."

"Not unusual," Farouche said. "I myself served with Arabs whose forefathers fought against French forces in North Africa." He studied Swift Elk for another few minutes, then suddenly turned toward Falconi. "I must tend to some matters now, *mon colonel.*" He checked his watch. "With your permission, I would like to have a formal meeting with you and your officers in my quarters this evening."

"Of course," Falconi said. "That will be with my two team leaders. That includes Swift Elk here."

"*Bien,*" Farouche said. He saluted, then made an abrupt turn and walked away. He walked toward the village square and found the man who was waiting for him there. It was his second-in-command. "Ming," he called to him.

Ming, who had been conferring with several subordinate unit leaders, took his leave of them and joined his commander. "Yes, commandant?"

"It appears our plans will be more complicated than expected," Farouche said. "The Americans have developed operational procedures in unconventional warfare that surpass those under which I operated."

"What do you mean, commandant?"

"They have posted guards, Ming. That means they do not trust us," Farouche said. "If we are to kill them, we must first put them at ease. That means going out on combat operations with them a few times."

"Good idea, commandant," Ming said enthusiastically.

"It is obvious from what le Colonel Falconi tells me that they will not order any supplies in until they are certain our efforts will help their cause in Southeast Asia."

Ming assumed a worried expression. "But, commandant! That means we will have to fight Viet Minh forces. We do not even know where they are."

"Correction, Ming. They are not Viet Minh anymore. They are North Vietnamese."

"What are North Vietnamese?" Ming asked.

"I'll explain later. At any rate, we don't need them. We can fight our enemies in the opium wars and tell le colonel Falconi they are Red partisans or irregulars."

"I think that will work, commandant. But we can't let them interrogate any prisoners," Ming warned him.

"This is not going to be easy," Farouche said. "Yet, if we are careful, we shall succeed handsomely."

"Yes, commandant."

"I want you to get Sari for me."

Ming grinned. "You have decided you cannot live without her beauty, commandant?"

"I want her for Falconi," Farouche said. "If she loves me as much as she says, she will not hesitate to spy for me. Even if it means she beds with another man."

79

"The woman is mad for you, commandant," Ming assured him. "She will be honored to serve you."

"Fetch her quickly, then," Farouche said. "In a little while I shall put my plan into operation. Is the intelligence on Liu's gang current?"

"Yes, commandant. The planned attempt to move a quantity of opium through our territory is still in the works."

"Good! That will be our first action as comrades-in-arms with the Americans," Farouche said. "Now. *Vite!* Get the girl. I must brief her before the staff meeting I have arranged with Falconi and his officers."

Lantern light flickered through Farouche's quarters throwing dancing shadows across the bamboo walls and up to the thatched roof.

Farouche inhaled a cigarette taken from the pack that Falconi had given him. "These American smokes are *magnifique*. Much better than those harsh Chinese type I've been forced to endure for so long."

Falconi, Chris Hawkins, and Ray Swift Elk occupied chairs in a semicircle around the Frenchman. "We will order some more in on the first supply drops," Falconi promised.

"Ah, yes, most generous, *mon colonel*," Farouche said. "And I desire very much to discuss supplies." He pulled his Chinese pistol from his holster and showed it to the Americans. "This is a cheap copy of the Russian Tokorev. I would like very much to have an American .45. My men also have Chinese AK47s that are not as reliable as the Soviet models. Perhaps rifles like yours." He pointed to the one that Swift Elk held between his knees. "I have never seen that kind before."

"They are called M16s," Swift Elk explained. "Five fifty-six millimeter. They have selectors which make them either semi- or full-automatic."

"*Fantastique!*" Farouche exclaimed. "I have never heard of such a weapon. When I first arrived here I carried a MAT 49 submachine gun. It was quite good—9-millimeter—but it wore out and I could get no ammunition for it anyhow."

"We are evaluating the arms situation," Falconi said diplomatically. "When your needs have been properly determined, then we shall request a supply drop as quickly as possible."

Farouche reholstered his pistol and leaned forward in his chair. "And when will that be?"

Chris Hawkins interjected. "We must study your operations, Sergeant Farouche. At that time we—"

"Do not refer to me as sergeant," Farouche interrupted. "I am known as commandant. Understood?"

"Of course," Chris said in his best upper-class New England manner. "And I apologize. I certainly didn't mean any insult."

"It is all right, *mon lieutenant*," Farouche said. "Please continue."

"As I was saying, we can only determine your exact needs from seeing what sort of operations and missions you conduct," Chris said.

"We must also study your enemy in the area," Swift Elk added.

Farouche smiled at the Sioux. "I like you. You talk like a sergeant."

"I am a sergeant," Swift Elk said. "A master sergeant."

"Ah! *Sergent chef*, eh?"

"That's correct," Swift Elk said. "When do you think we can participate in an operation against the enemy?"

"In the morning," Farouche said.

The three Black Eagles hid the surprise they felt. Falconi remained cool. "What sort of a fight will we be going into?"

81

"An ambush," Farouche answered. "I have received word of this opportunity only within the last hour." He consulted his watch. "As a matter of fact, we should be leaving within fifteen minutes if we hope to be set up before dawn."

Falconi glanced at his men. "It was nice you brought that into the conversation."

Farouche got up and went to his liquor cabinet. "Let's have a drink now. We'll toast our favorite diversion—*la guerre*—may it come often, and last a long, long time!"

CHAPTER 8

The birds and insects in the jungle glen resumed their normal activities an hour after the alien human males settled themselves into the area.

Normally, this would not have happened. The activities of the interlopers would have been disruptive enough to keep the natural denizens disturbed into silence. But these particular men went undercover and became as still as death. They made only the most necessary of movements, and when they spoke or communicated with each other it was in quiet whispers and subtle gestures. They blended with the vegetation so skillfully and completely that the only way the animals sensed their presence was the man-odor that could not be concealed.

Although the activity seemed soothing and peaceful enough, the animals could not comprehend that the visitors into their environment were there on a deadly purpose. Exactly as the leopard awaits his unsuspecting prey, these men were waiting for their own victims to make an appearance. But, unlike that great hunting cat, this particular group were going to kill those of their own species.

The Black Eagles, strung out along the trail they covered, had Farouche's men intermingled among them. Swift Elk's Bravo Fire Team was at the rear of the ambush. Their job would be to close in that portion of the fighting zone when the first shot was fired. That way no escapee could slip away to bring up reinforcements or report the battle.

Fire Team Alpha, under Chris Hawkins, was positioned at the front. Their job was similar to the Bravos', except that they would seal in the victims in the forward area of the battle.

Robert Falconi, Archie Dobbs, and Chief Brewster were in the center of the formation with Farouche and his men. Falconi noticed that the Frenchman was relaxed, almost nonchalant as the group waited for the people they were to ambush. Lucien Farouche even slept a bit, though he awoke after only brief moments of sleep each time he dozed off.

This entire effort was based on information that Farouche's sources had supplied them. The intelligence, which Falconi was forced to trust under the circumstances, described the enemy force as a small column of two dozen men moving food supplies to other Red partisans and militia to the west. It was determined that keeping these rations from the enemy would cause a breakdown in Communist activities among peaceful Meo tribesmen who were being terrorized by these invaders of their ancestral homelands.

The Black Eagles and their own Meo allies had left Faroucheville early the previous evening. The perilous and slow trek down jungle trails to the ambush site had taken the entire night. Everyone was worn out and in a bad temper as team leaders of both groups assigned positions and firing zones.

Only Archie Dobbs, irrepressibly eager and enthusiastic, displayed any good humor. He even asked permission to scout farther up the trail toward the area from which the enemy would be approaching. But Falconi vetoed that and made the detachment scout settle down to wait like everybody else.

The sun was forty-five degrees off the earth's surface when Falconi checked his watch. He leaned close to Farouche, who lay concealed on the pungent jungle earth beside him. "I thought those guys were supposed to show up a little past dawn. What the hell could have happened?"

Farouche shrugged. "*Qui sait?* Our war here is not so sophisticated as yours, *mon colonel*. Time and distances are judged in primitive perspective by uncivilized minds. But if my source is completely trustworthy—provided he has been bribed properly—and if he says the *merdes* are going to be here, they will be here."

"How about arithmetic?" Falconi asked. "He said a couple of dozen. Can we depend on that?"

Farouche laughed softly. "*Mais non!* Of course not. That is what is fun about fighting out here. So many things are unexpected."

"It makes solid planning a bit difficult, doesn't it?"

"Of course, *mon colonel*," Farouche replied. "But that is why we need so much in supplies. With mortars, demolitions, radios, and other modern gear, we could meet any situation the enemy could throw at us."

"I'll make a note of that," Falconi said.

The two stopped speaking and silence once again settled over the small valley.

The man closest to the enemy's approach was Blue Richards. The Alabama navy seal, with green and black stripes of camouflage paint across his face, lay prone under a palm bush. He listened with all the alertness of a hungry wolf for any alien sounds approaching. Every nerve was like a live electric wire, the tenseness causing momentary muscle cramps between his shoulders.

Suddenly, after hours of waiting, he heard a small, distant crack of sound.

Blue closed his eyes as if that would increase his faculties for sound. There was nothing but silence and the occasional chirp of a bird or the buzz of a flying insect.

Then he discerned a soft crunch some ways off.

This was it. Blue made a quick, clicking sound with his tongue on the roof of his mouth.

Doc Robichaux heard it and made a little wave of his hand to Dwayne Simpson. Dwayne silently passed the word up to Ray Swift Elk. The Sioux could see Archie Dobbs in his own hidden position, and he sent the signal on.

Within twenty seconds all the Black Eagles, from Blue in the rear all the way to Paulo Garcia, the most forward man, were aware that the objects of their lethal attention were drawing near.

Five minutes after the silent communications, Blue sighted the first of the bad guys. The fellow was not particularly alert, but from the way he carried his AK47, it was obvious he knew there was at least some potential for trouble. The man wore no uniform, only the dark pajama-like suit so prevalent among the Meo hill people. A red turban was wrapped around his head and he sported a haversack over his shoulder and an ammo belt around his waist.

Blue instinctively hugged closer to the ground as the man walked by. There were supposed to be twenty-four men in the column. The plan was for the Bravos to let them all through, then close in on the rear. The ambush had been laid out so that Paulo Garcia, upon sighting that first man, could blow the bastard away a couple of beats after the last man entered the combat area.

Blue counted on. He reached twenty-three, twenty-four, twenty-five, twenty-six—

Up ahead, Paulo could easily hear the approach of his target. He raised his rifle and waited.

Meanwhile Blue, becoming more than just a bit worried, continued to count as the enemy column trudged past his position. Thirty-two, thirty-three, thirty-four. He desperately hoped the last man would appear. If not, and there were plenty yet to come, Paulo's shot would herald the opening of an all-out attack, not an ambush.

Thirty-eight, thirty-nine, forty, forty-one—

Up ahead Paulo saw his man and squeezed the trigger. The guy's red turban flew off as he spun around under the impact of the bullet. Paulo fired again, then the whole area erupted into a roaring fire fight.

Now Blue swung into action. But instead of closing in from the rear as originally planned, he had to fire into a large group of enemy now storming the position. He fired on full auto to discourage the front attackers, and backed toward the rest of the team.

"This way! This way!" he yelled. "There's fifty more o' them fuckers comin' in on us!"

Doc Robichaux waited for Blue to pull back to him, then he began firing into the attacking enemy. Swift Elk and Dwayne Simpson had to contend with several baddies who had been allowed to pass by Blue. These guys responded with their Chinese AK47s, spewing out bursts of slugs into the jungle on both sides of the trail.

Two of Farouche's Meos caught fusillades in the torso and they went down after having fired only a couple of shots. But their nearby comrades added their own firepower to the Black Eagles' efforts.

Things looked damn good up at the front. Within a short matter of ten seconds all the enemy who had penetrated the ambush position were down wounded or dead. Under the original plan, this should have happened to all the Reds, but since they numbered many more than had been reported, a good-sized attack had built up in the rear where Swift Elk and his Bravos fought frantically against an attack that was mounting in strength.

Farouche wasn't particularly disturbed. He was used to things going to hell because of unreliable intelligence. The Frenchman simply yelled, *"En avant!"*

His Meos let out piercing, shrill screams and ran toward the growing battle in the rear. They collided with Swift Elk's men who were making a hasty, but strategic withdrawal under heavy pressure.

The four Black Eagles of Bravo Team were rock-and-rolling on full auto, their skillfully measured bursts of six and seven bullets sweeping back and forth into the bodies of the attackers. Although they were throwing plenty of hurt into the Reds, they were still forced to pull back. Only their compact, spaced fusillades allowed them the luxury of getting the hell out of that deadly hornets' nest.

The Meos, in their eagerness to attack, ruined all this. Still yelling in a fanatical frenzy, they bumped against the Black Eagles, then ran out into their field of fire to force the fight into hand-to-hand.

It was an incredibly stupid thing to do.

The attackers blew them off their feet into a pile of bloody meat, then pressed on toward the main formation. Swift Elk, never a man to use flowery phrases or overstatement, gave his orders in a loud, crisp voice:

"Haul ass!"

The Bravos moved back a few meters, but were again hindered when more of Farouche's Meos hemmed them in. Forced into a fight they didn't want, the Black Eagle fire team did what they had to do. The desperate men flung themselves into the brush on either side of the trail and fought for their lives.

The attackers, their rolling momentum in their favor, came on confidently. The only area of maneuver was the jungle track, and they used their packed formation to fullest advantage. The muzzles of their assault rifles pointed forward like porcupine quills and blasted hails of bullets forward and into the brush.

Swift Elk ducked and cursed as the fronds he was using for cover disintegrated into green powder as hundreds of bullets zipped through it.

But at that precise time, Falconi led the Command Element into the fight. Instead of a wild, useless attack like the Meos', he directed a coordinated effort that included hurling three hand grenades over the first rank of Reds. The deadly devices landed in the midst of the enemy formation and exploded with a roaring blast of flying shrapnel.

This didn't stop the front rank of the assault, but the mangled bodies in the center discouraged the hell out of those pressing in from the rear.

Falconi, now with the Alpha Fire Team in tow, went straight in with M16s blazing. Farouche and some of his best men who were with him, made this new element over twenty strong. Their combined firepower swept away the enemy's vanguard, leaving the twitching bodies of the dead and the writhing wounded in bloody piles.

Swift Elk leaped up as Falconi and the others raced past. He signaled the Bravo Team to follow, and they joined the deadly effort. They leaped over the mangled corpses of the grenade victims, and the battle peaked to a final stand, with so much roaring and firing that the concussion shook the limbs of the trees overhead.

"Cease fire!" Falconi ordered.

"*Cessez le feu!*" Farouche echoed.

Falconi glanced around for his team leaders. "Report."

"No casualties," Chris said.

"Okay in the Bravos, too," Swift Elk added.

Farouche didn't give a damn about his own dead and wounded. Instead he walked on the bodies of the fallen foe as he searched out their cargo. Finally he found the wicker baskets that several of them had been carrying coolie-style across their shoulders on poles. He yelled back at Ming who sent several of the Meo forward to gather up the loot.

Falconi motioned to Chris. "Take your guys on up forward and set up for security." He tapped Archie on the shoulder. "Take a look farther down the trail. I don't want any more of the little bastards sneaking up on us."

"Yes, sir," Archie said. Happy to get away from the crowd and out on his own, he rushed to the assignment. He passed Farouche and glanced down at the baskets, then went farther out into the jungle.

Falconi yelled out at the Frenchman. "What kind of loot was there?"

Farouche held up his hands in a gesture of surprise. "*Que pensez-vous?* That part of the intelligence we received was correct. There are field rations here. I will take them for my own men. What is that saying in English? Waste not, want not?"

Falconi nodded. "Good idea."

While some of the Meos gathered up the cargo baskets, Farouche ordered the others to begin another task. The tribesmen inspected the fallen enemy. They turned each over and removed his weapon and ammunition.

A shot blasted in the area. Then another, and another.

"What the hell's going on?" Falconi demanded.

"Nothing important," Farouche said walking up to him. "My men are shooting the Viet Minh wounded."

Falconi didn't bother to correct his terminology from Viet Minh to Viet Cong, but he nearly lost control of his temper. His voice quaked, however, as he spoke. "Don't you think it would be a good idea to save one or two for questioning?"

Farouche's face remained impassive. "No, *mon colonel.*" He turned and walked away, then stopped. He looked back at Falconi. "And you, Monsier le Colonel Falconi, don't you think it would be a good idea to get us some more supplies?"

Falconi maintained the rigid control of his anger. "Okay, Farouche. I'll agree with you on that. But it's not going to be that simple. There's still a hell of a lot to take into consideration before any final decisions are made."

"You are a very serious officer, *mon colonel*."

"I always am when I go to war," Falconi said.

Farouche smiled and saluted. *"Vive la guerre!"*

CHAPTER 9

Lucien Farouche pushed the cover down on the receiver of his Chinese AK47 assault rifle and snapped it closed. He worked the bolt several times to make sure there was no round in the chamber. Next he pulled the trigger of the freshly oiled and cleaned weapon and set it aside.

After putting away ramrod, patches, and other cleaning gear, he wiped his smudged hands on a rag. When he was satisfied he'd cleaned away most of the lubricant, he settled back in his chair and picked up the scotch and soda sitting on the table by his elbow. Farouche took a pensive sip and relaxed with the drink. He allowed the liquor's effect to melt away the tensions from the fight at the ambush site. This was his standard practice after returning to his quarters following an operation. Farouche wouldn't touch opium for the world, but he was one hell of a devotee to alcohol.

The trip back from the ambush site had been uneventful, except for having to be careful not to let Monsieur le Colonel Falconi or his men see the bricks of dried opium that had been looted from the dead enemy. The dark brown substance had been carefully and quickly wrapped up in palm fronds, as normal rations would have been. This was done under Ming's careful supervision while Farouche carried on an animated critique of the mission with the American commander and his two senior subordinates. His loud talk and wild gesturing had been more to distract the Americans than to emphasize the points he was trying to make in the conversation.

After the narcotics were ready for transport—still in the guise of rations—the column moved back to Faroucheville on the double.

Farouche, now with his boots off, lit one of the American cigarettes that Falconi had given him. The damned thing was delicious to the European. As an enlisted man, he'd smoked cheap French brands before his isolation in the Asian wilds. After his insertion into the original G.M.I. operation area, he had been forced to endure even worse varieties produced in the Orient. Tobacco and alcohol were the two vices he allowed himself. Farouche was too smart to even try narcotics. He had seen too many dumb-ass opium and heroin addicts ever to tempt that particular living hell. A couple he'd been acquainted with had been white men, too. One was an Australian adventurer who had gotten into drug smuggling, and the other was the Aussie's partner, a German deserter from the French Foreign Legion. Both had succumbed to the living death they had been shipping out to the free world. The last time Farouche had seen the German he was lying dead from an overdose, and his final sight of the Australian had been of a living skeleton reduced to menial, degrading labor for other smugglers in order to feed his insidious habit.

Farouche finished his scotch and got up to mix another. He'd just returned to his chair when a loud knock on the door caught his attention. *"Oui?"*

"C'est moi, Ming," his chief lieutenant answered. "We are here, commandant."

Farouche settled down into the chair once more. "Come in."

Ming entered with the woman Sari at his side. She smiled in a hopeful manner. The joy that was in her heart danced through her eyes. "Hello, *chéri*," Sari said.

Ming gave her a small shove toward the Frenchman. "Do you require any more of me, commandant?"

"No, my friend," Farouche said. He waited until the man left. "I had wanted to talk to you sooner, but didn't get the chance. Come closer to me, Sari."

"Of course, *chéri*," she said. The small woman, her beauty as fragile as that of a jungle orchid, padded forward on her bare feet. She wore a sarong wrapped tight around her lithe body. Knowing exactly what lit Farouche's fire of passion, she had arranged the garment to show off her cleavage. There was a slit up one side that displayed tantalizing flashes of upper thigh. Each step she took, with a slight undulation of the hips, played up her natural sensuousness to its best advantage.

"Why do you call me *chéri*?" Farouche asked.

"Because you taught me that it means 'darling' in the language of France," Sari said.

"That is correct," Farouche said. "But is that the only reason you call me that?"

"I do so because I love you, *chéri*," Sari said with great feeling. Tears welled gently in her eyes and one trickled slowly down her cheek. "You are my life!" she said passionately. "You know that, *chéri*! Deep in your heart, you must!"

Farouche yawned. "Words are cheap. All the women who have pleasured me here have spoken to me of their love."

Sari moved a few steps forward and fell to the floor. She continued toward him on her knees until finally she fell at Farouche's feet. "No woman could want you or cherish you with the same strength in their heart as me, *chéri*!" she exclaimed. "You must believe me!"

"I want to believe you," Farouche said. "But I feel the women who want me only do so in order to enjoy the luxuries I can shower on them."

"Oh, not me, *chéri!*" Sari cried.

The Frenchman drained this second drink and handed her the glass. "Fetch me another."

"Of course, *chéri*," Sari said happily. She got to her feet and scurried over to the liquor cabinet to mix him a drink exactly as he liked it. She returned to him and gave him the scotch and soda, then once again fell to the floor.

Farouche drank slowly, studying the girl for several minutes before he spoke. "I demand proof of your love," he said finally.

"Yes, *chéri!*" Sari exclaimed. "I will do anything!"

"The first thing you can do is stop that *chéri* shit," Farouche said.

"It is the only French word of endearment I know," Sari said, ashamed. Then her expression brightened. "Teach me another!"

"Very well," Farouche said yawning. "Use *mon amour.* That means 'my love.'"

"Yes, *mon amour*," Sari said stumbling a bit over the unfamiliar words. "Tell me what you want of me."

"You have seen the Americans who have come to fight with us?" Farouche asked.

"Of course, *mon amour*," Sari answered.

"And you have noted their leader?"

"He is the tall one, no?"

"That is him," Farouche said. "He is supposed to be my friend—my comrade-in-arms—but I do not trust him."

Sari hissed through her small white teeth. "Then kill him, *mon amour!*"

Farouche shrugged. "But if he is indeed my friend, then it would be a shame." He reached out and gently touched her hair. "I must find out exactly what he thinks of me."

Sari, finding his caresses exquisite, sighed in contentment. "Your touch moves me so!"

Farouche became blunter. "I want you to find out all about him."

Sari's eyes opened in puzzlement. "But how, *mon amour*? If a man as intelligent and wise as you cannot, what can I do? I am only a foolish woman."

"You are a woman," the Frenchman said flatly.

The full meaning of what he was after dawned on her. Sari held out her hands in an imploring gesture. "Oh, no, *mon amour*. Do not make me do this. I could not bear to have another man touch me."

"Go to the American," Farouche commanded her. "Make love to him and gain his confidence. I want you to find out everything you can about him and his men, then report back to me through Ming."

"Don't ask me to do this!" Sari begged.

"Only if you make this sacrifice will I believe in your love," Farouche said. The Frenchman knew this might not be enough inducement even for Sari, so he added, "and when this is all over I will make you my wife."

"Oh, *mon amour*!" she cried. "I had only hoped to be your favorite concubine. But to be your wife!"

"You will do it, then?" Farouche asked.

Sari nodded and smiled. "Within a few weeks, there will be nothing I do not know about the American colonel or his men."

"Start tonight," Farouche said. "But in the meantime, get me another drink."

Sari quickly complied and returned to him with a properly mixed scotch and soda. "Do you have anything else you wish to ask of me, *mon amour*?"

"Yes," Farouche answered. "How about mixing up those *mon amour* and *chéris*? Hearing the same one over and over will drive me mad."

Falconi lit a cigarette and slowly exhaled. He glanced across the table and looked meaningfully at Chris Hawkins and Ray Swift Elk in the lantern light that danced across the hut they used as headquarters. "I want a couple of quick evaluations on the Frenchman. And I mean military judgments on his character and capabilities."

Chris Hawkins leaned back in his chair. "A capable guy and a good soldier," he said. "Unlike many European noncommissioned officers, this guy can think on his feet. He's unconventional and too careless, but that has probably been to his advantage because of the peculiarity of the warfare he's been conducting. What I mean to say, is that this guy hasn't been fighting a civilized enemy in a conventional situation. If I were to give him the benefit of any doubt, I'd say he's a bit out of touch."

"Right," Falconi said. He nodded to the Sioux Indian. "Okay, Swift Elk. Sound off."

"I'm a trained professional soldier," Swift Elk said. "But deep in my heart I'm a warrior like my ancestors. It's inbred in me to look upon war as a ritual of sorts, full of taboos and customs. That's why I decorate my face only in certain sacred patterns, even with camo paint. From deep within my psyche, I peer out as a Sioux brave, and I can judge Lucien Farouche on that level."

"That's a hell of a unique observation," Falconi said. "So, what do you think of him?"

"He's crazier'n a fucking loon," Swift Elk said.

Both Falconi and Chris laughed. Falconi almost dropped his cigarette. "Go on. Explain yourself."

Swift Elk smiled at them. "Okay. Okay. I'll admit I can get melodramatic sometimes. But this guy is probably like the white trappers and hunters that moved among the Indians in our own country. They fit in well, didn't get too pushy, and took local wives. But after a time of combining their white ways with Indian ways, things got mixed up for them. In the end they didn't fit into any world very well. They really weren't Indians, and they could never live among genteel whites again."

"In other words," Falconi surmised, "You think Farouche has been out in the boondocks too long, huh?"

"Yes, sir," Swift Elk said.

"If I don't use that benefit of doubt I mentioned, sir," Chris said, "I'd have to agree with Swift Elk."

"Well, that couldn't be all that bad," Falconi said. "Hell, we don't want to get him back to Saigon or Paris anyhow. We want him to stay out here and keep up the good fight."

Chris shrugged. "In all candor I must say that I think in the end he'll turn out okay."

"Agreed, sir," Swift Elk said. "But there's something about the guy that really bothers me."

Falconi eyed Swift Elk. "You sound like you've got more to say."

"Not really," Swift Elk said. "But I do think we ought to test him again. Maybe on something a bit more substantial than an ambush."

"I'll go along with that," Chris remarked.

Falconi stood up and walked to the door of the hut. He flipped the cigarette out into the dark, letting his mind mull over what his two team leaders were saying. After a few minutes he returned to the table. "If the guy is really on the up-and-up and a capable leader, he'll be invaluable to the war effort. On the other hand, if he's a flake we can end up wasting a lot of time and good equipment that could be used elsewhere."

"Not to mention getting a few guys zapped, colonel," Swift Elk added.

"That's something you don't have to tell me," Falconi said. "I've got the figures right here." He tapped his forehead. "There's been a total of forty-seven men who have either served or are serving in this detachment."

"Right, sir," Chris said. "And thirty-three of 'em have bought the farm."

"That's about a seventy percent casualty rate," Swift Elk added.

"I sure as hell don't want to make it a hundred percent," Falconi said.

"Then what's the plan?" Swift Elk asked.

"We'll draw Farouche into a big operation like we've talked about. If it looks like he can cut the mustard, we'll bring in some supplies and really go to town on this operation," Falconi said.

"And if he don't measure up?" Swift Elk asked.

"We'll have to pull out."

"He'll try to wipe us out, sir," Chris protested. "And if we attempt to strike first, we'll have a couple of thousand Meo tribesmen on our ass."

"In that case, gentlemen," Falconi said unemotionally, "You'd better hope like hell Farouche can fill the ticket." He glanced at his watch. "I'm going to get some sack drill."

"Me too," Swift Elk said. "But I'll look in on the guys first."

"Right," Falconi said. "I'll see you two in the morning." He left the headquarters hut and walked slowly down the dark village street to his own hut. He didn't bother to light a lantern when he got there. Instead, after shoving his Colt automatic under the pillow, the colonel undressed quickly to avoid insect bites and hurried under the mosquito netting arranged over his bamboo cot. He'd just settled down when he noted a movement outside his quarters. Falconi reached for the Colt .45 and raised it toward the shadow that now approached him through the door.

"Monsieur le colonel," a soft feminine voice said.

Falconi didn't let the weapon waver. "Yes?"

The woman came up to the bed. She stepped inside the netting and knelt on the bed. "I am Sari."

"I am Robert," Falconi said. His eyes were now used to the dark and he could easily see her even in the faint moonlight that streamed in from the thatched roof.

"I have been sent to be your woman," Sari said. She

slowly undid her long sarong and let it slip down.

Falconi felt his manhood stirring at the sight of the small uplifted, firm breasts. Her thighs seemed to flow up to her belly with the grace a sculptor might give a sensuous statue. He reached out and felt their softness, and the women leaned down to him. "Do you find me *belle*— beautiful?"

Falconi, suddenly remembering the pistol, deftly set it on the floor out of sight in the shadows. "Yes, Sari. You are a beautiful woman."

Sari kissed him, then lay down beside him. She gently pushed him above her, then gritted her teeth as she anticipated gyrating, pushing thrusts into her body.

Instead his warm hands caressed her, and he gently kissed her nipples, teasing them with his tongue. To her surprise, she felt some amount of pleasure in this, and was again surprised when he finally took her.

There was no pain. Only a gentle rocking inside her as a strange feeling of passion built slowly to a crest. Before Sari realized what was happening, she was grasping at the muscular male body with both her arms and legs as the pleasure finally peaked, and a feeling of contentment and fulfillment filled her.

A few minutes later, they lay side by side. Sari had regained control of herself. She took a deep breath as the warmth she had felt in her heart was replaced by cold calculation.

It was time to begin spying for her real lover.

100

CHAPTER 10

The Black Eagle Detachment's enlisted men, formed up into one rank of eight men, faced Master Sergeant Swift Elk. They were drawn up on Faroucheville's principal street just outside their quarters. Curious Meo inhabitants looked up from their daily activities to carefully eye these deadly strangers who had literally dropped into their midst. They were particularly fascinated by the tall, imposing, and near-savage handsomeness of Swift Elk.

The Sioux top kick had a clipboard holding a pad of scribbled notes. He ignored his gawking audience as he addressed the unit. "Awright," he said, "first thing is guard duty. We been pretty informal, but from now on sentry duty is gonna be done by teams. Chief Brewster will go with the Alphas and Archie with the Bravos for this job. That'll make four guys in each unit."

"Mmmm," Paulo Garcia mused. "That leaves out three guys, mainly two officers and—"

"—and one master sergeant who is me," Swift Elk said completing the sentence. "As Chief Brewster would say, I'd love to stand watch with you, shipmates, but higher duties and responsibilities call me away from your charming company."

There were good-natured catcalls from the others.

101

"RHIP—Rank Has Its Privileges—right, Ray?" Archie sang out.

"That's right," Swift Elk said. "But that ain't the only so-called privileges around here." He paused and grinned at his pals. "It looks like we're gonna be getting some attention from the local ladies."

The other Black Eagles cheered. Only Archie Dobbs looked uncomfortable.

"The Meos have fought with us," Swift Elk continued, "and feel that our happy group is like brothers now. They're sorry we gotta lay around them huts without proper female companionship, so the Falcon tells me we'll be getting married informally on a temporary basis."

"Not me!" Archie exclaimed.

All eyes turned incredulously toward the soldier who was reputed to be the horniest man in the United States Army. Blue Richards, standing beside the detachment scout, nudged him. "What's the matter with you, Archie? You got religion all of a sudden or what?"

"Hell, no," Archie said. "I got my Betty Lou." He was referring to his girl friend, who was an army nurse at the hospital in Long Binh.

"You cain't insult these folks," Blue cautioned him.

"I ain't being untrue to my own sweet love," Archie insisted.

Swift Elk sneered at him. "We'll worry about that when we see you turn down some available pussy."

This time the ribbing was aimed at Archie. "A hard-on ain't got no conscience," Hank Valverde said.

"Okay, knock it off. We'll let Archie wrestle with his own moral problems without any interference from us," Swift Elk said. "Anyhow, I ain't finished talking with you guys. The next thing we got going is a clinic. Doc Robichaux is going to give the local folks that want it a medical check-up, and we'll see about any necessary treatment. He may need some help with the paperwork, so keep yourselves ready for an extra detail."

Hank Valverde held up his hand. "What about resupply, Ray? Nobody's told me nothing one way or the other. Am I supposed to call in some stuff or not? And if so, when?"

"We'll be deciding that in a coupla days," Swift Elk answered. He looked over at Chief Brewster. "How's commo?"

"I been running checks ever'day," the navy chief answered. "Ever'thing's ship shape. Hell, we're so high up I could talk with Pearl Harbor if I wanted to."

"Good," Swift Elk said. "Now listen up, guys. Follow the guard roster, keep outta trouble, and treat the ladies nice. I understand they'll be dropping by for a visit this afternoon. You take your choices but show some class and consideration, huh?"

"Who are these beauties, anyhow?" Frank Matsamura asked.

"Some unattached females that are literally up for grabs," Swift Elk explained. "But that don't mean you treat 'em like cheap whores, hear? This is part o' these people's culture, and even if it seems kinda strange to our way o' thinking, display a lot of respect and mind your manners." He winked and lowered his voice. "The Old Man has got a real looker. A cute little number named Sari."

There was a burst of approving laughter from the Black Eagles.

"Good for the Falcon," Archie said. "He's got to learn to lighten up some."

"Don't worry, Swift Elk," Dwayne Simpson said. "We'll be perfect gentlemen."

"Fine," Swift Elk said. "In the meantime, me and the Falcon and Chris got a meeting with Farouche to discuss the situation at length. As soon as something is decided or planned, I'll let you know. Chief Brewster is in charge of the Alpha Fire Team, and Blue is gonna honcho the

Bravos."

"Shit!" Paulo yelled out. "The fucking navy has been put in charge of us."

"Life is a bitch," Swift Elk said. "Team leaders, take charge. I gotta go to a staff meeting."

The Indian left the men as they broke up into their two groups. He hurried across the village to the headquarters hut where Falconi and Chris Hawkins waited for him. He dropped off the clipboard. "The guys are squared away," he announced. "Doc Robichaux will have the clinic this afternoon."

"Good," Falconi said. "Let's make that call on Farouche and see where we'll go from here."

Chris was not optimistic. "This situation could turn ugly, or even dangerous."

"Yeah," Swift Elk said. "And to complicate matters, we're a hell of a long way from home."

"Nobody said this job would be easy," Falconi remarked. He strode in long, quick strides, with the other two only a step behind him. The trio walked up to the guards in front of Farouche's big house and stopped.

The sentries, ready for the visit, hurriedly opened the front door and admitted them. Ming was standing directly inside the foyer. He was polite but a bit severe as he saluted, then beckoned them to follow him down the hall. At Farouche's quarters, he stopped and opened the door for them.

"The commandant awaits you," Ming said.

"Thank you," Falconi said.

Farouche was evidently in an agitated mood. Fully dressed in his khaki uniform complete with boots and pistol belt, he turned and faced his visitors. "It is time," he said, "for some serious talking."

"We couldn't agree more," Falconi said.

"Sit down, messieurs," Farouche said. He gestured to three chairs he had arranged in a semicircle around his own special one. "I am not going to waste a lot of time or breath."

"Neither will we," Falconi said as he and his two men took seats.

The Frenchman also settled down. "I want mortars, recoilless rifles, plastic explosive, and M16s for my men." He looked directly into Falconi's face, the challenge in his voice undeniable.

Falconi kept calm as he slowly shook his head. "Not yet, commandant."

"Sacre merde!" Farouche shouted in anger. "What do you want of me, *mon colonel*? I am conducting a war here, and you piddle bits and pieces of light weaponry at me. You are supposed to help my cause, *non*?"

"Of course," Falconi said. "And we were most favorably impressed by both you and your men at the ambush. It was a good proof of your skill and bravery as a soldier and leader." He paused. "But not quite enough."

"You want a big battle?" Farouche asked angrily. *"La bataille grande?"*

"Calm yourself, commandant," Falconi said. "We don't expect a major offensive, of course. But we would like to see an operation that requires some logistic support, a bit of extra planning, and some troop movement."

"Ha!" Farouche yelled standing up. "You shall have it, *mon colonel*! I will call in Ming with maps. I can show you a village where enemy militia is well dug in. It will be dangerous and tough, but well worth the risk if it will get me the big stuff I need to knock off my rivals."

"Knock off your rivals?" Swift Elk asked.

Farouche instantly regretted using the phrase. "Of course. My enemies—the Reds—the Communists." He smiled and shrugged. "Who else?"

Chris Hawkins was direct. "Are you involved in any politics in the area here, commandant?"

Farouche, an expression of hurt indignity dancing across

105

his face, stood up and spoke in an injured tone. "Monsieur le lieutenant, I serve France!"

Falconi saw that things might get out of control. He also stood up. "I salute you, commandant. Let us plan the attack that you suggest."

Farouche excitedly rubbed his hands together as he rushed to the door. He flung it open and shouted down the hall. "Ming! Ming! Bring me the maps of the northern sector! Quickly! Quickly!" He returned to his guests.

"How far north are we going?" Falconi asked.

"We will be so close to the international border that stray shots will go into China."

Doc Robichaux listened intently to the baby's heartbeat through his stethoscope. He was performing his duties so completely professionally that even the well-formed breasts of the infant's mother, easily visible through her thin cotton blouse, did not rouse him. Using his rudimentary but adequate knowledge of her language, he questioned the woman about the child. "Does he have diarrhea for a time, then is constipated?"

The woman nodded yes, then added meekly. "Yes, monsieur le docteur, and he vomits much, too."

Robichaux, whose value as a medical practitioner depended as much on reputation as results, did not correct her about addressing him as "mister doctor." He noted the baby was also suffering from edema in the face and his belly was swollen with water-bloat. "There seems to be much of this in the village."

The woman nodded energetically. "Yes. And not just the children, too."

Doc removed the stethoscope and assumed a thoughtful air. There was now no doubt in his mind about this sickness that plagued many residents of Faroucheville. It was a disease called fasciolopsiasis. It was caused by a parasite that encysted certain water plants that were popular for eating raw. Although the illness could be fatal, it was easy to treat. The Black Eagle medic immediately prescribed the drug crystalline hexylresorcinol, to be taken on empty stomachs first thing the following morning. After three days of this, he would administer a purgative in the form of sodium sulfate. It might mean a hell of a lot of people crapping in the village latrines at the same time, but the results would be worth the inconvenience and smell.

Doc continued working hard during the long afternoon. Most of the health complaints he dealt with were parasitical in nature. The people would have to be taught to cut down on the raw fish and vegetables that were a part of their diet, and they would also have to be urged to boil their drinking water.

There were also the usual sores, open ulcers, ringworm, untreated cuts, and other problems for the versatile navy corpsman to deal with. He handled each case with professional competency. Finally, after the last patient was seen, Doc took a detailed tour of the village to check out the general sanitation.

There was no doubt that Farouche had great influence on the populace. There was adequate drainage for rainwater, and all garbage and trash was picked up and burned twice daily. The latrines were military in nature and kept as insect free as possible with old-fashioned cleanliness. All in all, Doc Robichaux was pleased with what he saw.

The Cajun decided to call it a day toward early evening. He had begun to pack up his medical kit when he sensed someone standing in the doorway of the hut he had turned into a dispensary. Doc looked up and saw a man standing there with a child in his arms. It was one of the Meo who had fought so valiantly in the ambush a couple of days earlier.

Doc didn't need to make a close medical examination. He could readily tell that the young boy, who appeared to be about five years of age, was deathly ill. "Put him in on the table."

The man did as he was told, then stepped back to watch.

"Your son?" Doc asked.

The Meo nodded affirmatively.

Doc made an in-depth examination beginning with the vital signs and pulse, temperature, and breathing. Even that was bad. He went into a more complex inspection of his little patient, and it was almost an hour before he made his final diagnosis.

"Tapeworm," he said. He looked at the father. "How long has he been sick?"

"Five weeks," the Meo answered.

"Jesus Christ!" Doc exclaimed. "That's near the limit." He immediately got out his gear again and set up a saline enema. He administered it several times, each effort producing a vile, bloody discharge. As he worked, Doc took notice of the father. Although the man's face was impassive, it was evident that, deep in his heart, he was frantic with worry.

After the enemas, the boy began to vomit. Doc was now concerned with dehydration. He administered an antiemetic, then set up for intravenous antibiotics. The final step was a one-gram dose of niclosamide.

Doc looked at the father. "There's gonna be a hell of a lot of waiting around."

The Meo said nothing. Instead, he simply squatted down, a silent statement of patient endurance.

Doc continued his careful ministering and observation. An hour later, Archie Dobbs passed by to look in. "We missed you at chow, Doc. What's keeping you?"

"I got a pretty sick boy here," Doc answered.

Archie peered at the infant. "Jesus! That's too bad. Is there anything I can do, Doc?"

"I need a lantern," Doc said. "This kid is in the advanced state of acute tapeworm infection. His chances ain't good, and I'm gonna have to sit up with him."

"Sure," Archie said. "I'll be right back, Doc."

Fifteen minutes later, Doc and the father were both situated for many slow hours of hopeful waiting and ministration.

It was going to be a long night.

CHAPTER 11

Archie Dobbs pulled the map from his pocket and squatted down. He sat it on the ground in front of him and oriented it using his compass and the grid lines. He hoped like hell that all the marginal information on the large topographical foldout in front of him was accurate as he turned the arrangement to coincide with the declination diagram.

The chart was a Chinese one supplied by Farouche. He had handed it over with an apologetic air. "My original issues of *cartes militaires* wore out long ago," he explained. "I obtained this one, like all the others I now have, off the bodies of dead enemy officers."

There turned out to be no real problems, however, since Archie was expert enough to be able to recognize terrain features without being able to read the foreign writing that gave elevations and place names.

Archie looked up from his task and called out in a loud whisper. "Blue!"

Blue Richards appeared out of the jungle behind the scout. "Yeah, Archie?" he answered just as softly.

"Damned straight," Blue said. It was well known within the detachment that he was the best tree climber in the Black Eagles. Blue also claimed to hold that title for the entire state of Alabama. "What should I look for?"

110

"There oughta be a distinctive ridge off to the west there," Archie said, looking down at the map. "If you see it, point dead at it so's I can shoot an azimuth."

"You call, I haul," Blue intoned using the Black Eagle saying. He stripped off his rucksack and webb gear. After leaning his M16 against the tree, he shinnied up it. Within moments he pointed outward.

Archie got directly under the navy seal and lined up on the pointing arm. He brought up his compass and sighted through it to the crosshairs. "That's it," he said. "Two-Niner-Zero." He motioned Blue to descend from his perch. He then turned his attention back to the map to make a paper-reconnaissance of the necessary route to the objective. Meanwhile, Blue returned to mother earth, gathered up his gear, and moved off.

Falconi slipped up behind Archie and knelt down. The rest of the detachment, complete with their Meo counterparts, waited in a column to the rear. The colonel wiped at the sweat seeping down from the olive-drab bandana wrapped around his head. "How far does it look Archie?"

"About three kilometers, sir," Archie answered. "As near as I can figure from distances we been traveling, this here map is a typical military one-to-fifty-thousand scale."

"I hope you're right," Falconi said. "We've got to depend on you. Farouche's map-reading skills have gotten rusty over the years."

"The guy is going native, if he ain't already there," Archie said. "He's about as strange as them Meos. That must come from eating their weird chow."

Falconi shrugged. "Their food isn't all that strange. Fish, pork, and vegetables are perfectly all right. Though I admit I'm not too fond of the grub and insect portion of their menus."

"Maybe what they eat in the village ain't so bad," Archie admitted. "But their field rations have got to be far-out eating. I caught a glimpse of that stuff right after the

111

ambush. It was dehydrated chow, and looked all hard and black-looking like bricks."

"No shit?" Falconi remarked. "I'll have to check into that. A lot of native stuff is real nutritious."

"You can have my share," Archie said.

Falconi checked his watch. "We'd better get moving if we want to get in position for an attack on that village in the morning."

"Right, sir," Archie said. "Let's start this bunch rolling again." He got to his feet and glided through the vegetation as Falconi signaled the others to follow.

The unit had been moving since early dawn. Both the thick jungle and the need for caution kept their progress down to a crawl. Also, Archie Dobbs, as scout, had been struggling with the Chinese map as he sought the best route to their target.

The object of their planned attack had been described to them by Farouche as a village about half the size of Faroucheville. An estimated five hundred people lived there, with approximately seventy-five to a hundred combatives to deal with. A combination of Black Eagles and Meos brought their own strength to a hundred and five fighting souls, but two fighters had been left behind.

Doc Robichaux's treatment of the sick child had grown complicated. The little boy had barely responded to the medicine, so both the medic and the small patient's father had been allowed to remain in Faroucheville to continue the lifesaving struggles necessary for the kid's survival.

The rest of the small army had loaded their gear and moved out in the cool redness of dawn. Farouche and Ming gave directions as best they could, but the greater burden of land navigation fell on Archie Dobbs's capable shoulders. If the scout couldn't find the target hamlet, then no one could.

The going had been incredibly rough.

The weather was steamy with heat, and clouds of insects

would suddenly rise out of the bushes to bite and sting the men as they passed by. Because of the need to be silent, no one was able either to slap at the pests or even curse them aloud. It was just something that had to be endured, like the steepness of the terrain.

Thigh muscles ached and burned with the effort of constant climbing. The only consolation was the fact that the return trip would be downhill. The Meos, short and stocky, their asses low on their frames, had a natural center of gravity that made the tough terrain easy for them. But the Americans, despite their superb conditioning, worked hard as their longer muscles were required to contract more in the necessary movements to work their way higher into the mountains.

There was some silent, good-natured kidding about the suffering of the foreigners. Now and then, a couple of Meos would slip up behind a Black Eagle and lift the larger man up to help him along. When this happened to Chief Brewster, he grinned back at them. After they released him he hefted up the little men in his muscular arms and carried them fifty meters before setting them down again.

Finally, toward late afternoon, Archie signaled a halt. When both Falconi and Farouche joined him, he pointed to the ground. There was a barely discernible jungle trail, but a sandal-print, as obvious to the scout as a blinking neon sign, could be seen in the smashed grass.

"I'll make a recon, sir," Archie said. Without waiting for a confirming order, he slipped himself free of all his equipment. Moving forward with his .45 holstered, but a knife in one hand, Archie began the dangerous search for the actual location of the village.

Fifteen minutes later, crouched on a knoll, he looked down into a large depression to where a Meo village was located. It seemed the size that Farouche had described. Archie slipped the knife into the ground and pulled out a pad and pencil. He quickly sketched a map of the hamlet's layout, the immediate terrain around it, and the areas where most of the population was concentrated. When he had finished, Archie recovered the knife and moved back to the column.

Both Falconi and Farouche studied the map. The colonel thought it a good time to check out Farouche's tactical skill. "What do you think, commandant?"

"A three-pronged attack with the center carrying the most of it," Farouche said. "The area to the rear of the village looks like an impassable swamp. That will act as a fourth invisible 'squad.' It should be able to hem in escapees, or at least slow them up enough for us to be able to close in and wipe out any resistance." He looked into Falconi's eyes, a challenging smile dancing across his features. "*Bien*, what do you think, *mon colonel?*"

"I agree with you a hundred percent," Falconi said. "But let's remember there're noncombatants down there. Our first volleys of fire should be high enough to warn them off without hitting them."

Farouche assumed a merciful expression on his rugged face. "I, too, believe in the humane treatment of women and children in war, *mon colonel*."

"Good," Falconi said. "I'm glad we see eye to eye on that. Now, what time do you recommend we attack?"

"At dawn, of course," Farouche answered. "We can catch the bastards flat-footed that way."

"Again, I agree," Falconi said. Then he added diplomatically, "you will allow me to deploy my own troops, of course."

"*Mais oui*," Farouche said smiling. "And you will allow me to intersperse mine with yours, *non?*"

"Sure," Falconi said. He walked back toward the detachment with both the Frenchman and Archie trailing him. When they reached the other men, Falconi signaled them all to crowd around him. He displayed Archie's map.

"We're short one man and have three sides to cover," Falconi said. "So I'm going to break up our team integrity."

The Black Eagles took the unusual orders without an outward show of disappointment.

"Left flank," Falconi said, pointing to that side of the map. "Chris in command with Paulo and Hank. Swift Elk will take the right. Blue and Dwayne go with him. That leaves me, Chief Brewster, Archie, and Frank in the center."

"What's the general plan of action, sir?" Chris asked.

"The attack will be at dawn and will be launched from the center," Falconi said. "I want the preliminary fusillades to go high to scare off the noncombatants. Then you guys on the flank move in and secure your areas. It's simple, but it should do quite well in these circumstances. Hell, that's not exactly a concrete-and-steel fortification down there, just some sloppy grass huts."

"Aye, aye, sir," Chris said.

"Commandant Farouche will move his own men among us as was done at the ambush," Falconi added.

"And I personally will stay with you, *mon colonel*," Farouche said.

"An honor," Falconi said. He motioned to Chris and Swift Elk. "Take your men and position 'em. Stay on the alert through the night. We'll keep in contact by Prick-Six."

"If you will excuse me, *mon colonel*," Farouche said. "I must see to my own command."

Frank Matsamura separated himself from Alpha Team and joined the Command Element. "It looks like I'm coming up in the world," he remarked with a laugh.

"Sure," Archie said. "But it's lonely at the top, Frank."

Chief Brewster lit a cigarette. "It ain't gonna be lonely in the center of that attack in the morning," he cautioned them. "We'll be catching most of the attention." He paused as he exhaled a cloud of smoke. "There's a saying in the navy about such a situation."

Archie grinned. "What is it you swabbies say, Chief?"

"It's called going into harm's way," Chief responded. He wasn't grinning.

Doc Robichaux rubbed his red eyes and stared wearily past the flickering lantern out into the dark village street. Although he couldn't see them, he could sense the people waiting where they had been since early that morning.

The word of his trying to save the boy had spread fast among Faroucheville's population. The family concerned, as it should be, occupied the choicest site directly in front of the dispensary hut. The father, who had stuck it out through the entire night and the next day, squatted in silence by the door.

A couple of times, Doc thought the kid had given up the ghost. During one harrowing incident, when all breath ceased, the medic had applied mouth-to-mouth for a full half hour. Finally, the boy had gurgled and vomited. Doc quickly cleared the kid's throat and nose with his hand-suction device, and the youngster settled into labored but regular breathing.

Only then did the father speak. He got up and walked slowly over to his son. After staring down at him, he glanced at Doc. "Did you breath life into him?" he asked.

"You could say that," Doc said.

"He now has part of your soul in his body," the father said.

"I don't know for sure what he's got in there," Doc said. "But he sure as hell ain't got that tapeworm now." Hours before, the enemas had caused the expulsion of the slimy creature. Now all they could do was hope that whatever damage had been done to the boy had been undone. The navy seal corpsman had also discovered the real culprit behind the illness—trichinosis. Although in the developing stages, the tapeworm's insidious presence had so weakened the kid's resistance that he was fast succumbing. Doc had responded with extra-large doses of corticosteroids.

If he could convince the villagers to cook the hell out of their food instead of half-assed quick boiling or eating the stuff raw, Doc thought, he could solve half their health problems.

His mind whirling with the things he had to do as a medic, Doc finally slipped into sleep sitting on a stool. His head bobbed, then a sudden sound awoke him.

The child was crying.

Doc jumped up and rushed to him. The kid's eyes were wide and frightened, but he calmed down some when his father came over. Doc slipped his stethoscope on and listened to the little heart. The rhythm was regular and strong now. He touched the boy's forehead.

"The fever is gone!" Doc exclaimed happily.

"He is saved," the father said with solemn finality. His basic instincts told him that death was no longer hovering around the hut.

Doc grinned and nodded his head enthusiastically. "Yeah. I think that's a good prognosis. He's gonna live." He gently pulled the father away. "But he needs sleep. A lot of it, so his body can finish fighting off the infection."

"Yes, monsieur le docteur," the Meo said. "But he will not die now. He has a part of your soul in him."

Doc fetched a thermometer from the medical kit. "We'll use an oral one this time," he said winking. "We been shoving enough stuff up the little guy's ass."

The father didn't grin at the joke. "Do you understand?"

"Understand what?" Doc asked.

"My son has part of your soul," the father said. "That means neither of you will be whole in the afterworld until you both die."

"I'll wait for him," Doc said.

"If you take back your soul, he will die."

"I won't have it returned," Doc said. "I didn't work on him all night to do something like that."

The father stepped back and watched as a fresh bottle of antibiotics was arranged by the hardworking medical corpsman.

Later, as the night turned the jungle inky black, ten Black Eagles and fifty of Farouche's Meo tribesman passed the long, slow hours as the time of the attack approached with the deadly certainty of a languidly swimming tiger shark.

Archie Dobbs, wakeful, waited with Chief Brewster's words running over and over through his mind:

In harm's way.

CHAPTER 12

Dawn, like the sunset, is fast in the tropics. A small, pinkish glow on the horizon showed dimly through the trees. Despite this rather weak beginning, there was precious little time before full-blown daylight would break on the scene.

The ranking men of both the Black Eagles and Farouche's Meos immediately saw to it that all hands were wide awake and ready for the coming battle.

Lieutenant Colonel Robert Falconi, flanked by Archie Dobbs and Lucien Farouche, took enough time to peer at the objective through his binoculars in spite of the shortage of time. His magnified gaze swept the village and showed that the inhabitants were lethargically greeting the new day, only a few of them venturing outside their huts. These were mostly women, who went to the well to fetch water needed to prepare breakfasts.

Falconi stuck the binocs back in the carrier, and checked his watch. "It's time." He got to his feet and moved forward. Farouche, Archie Dobbs, Chief Brewster, and Frank Matsamura spread out slightly behind him in a "V" formation. As they burst out of the jungle and into the clear, the colonel raised his M16 and fired a high burst of automatic fire.

The rest of the attacking force did likewise, and the

women at the well screamed in horror. They rushed back to their huts. Some collided with their men, who emerged in sleepy anger and alarm. The surprise apparently wasn't as complete as they'd hoped. These villagers obviously always expected trouble. The males, despite the impolite awakening, were armed and ready for action.

The Black Eagles cut loose with some more high firing designed to drive the noncombatants out of the area and the fighting zone before the serious combat began.

But Farouche and his men, despite the Frenchman's assurances to Falconi, had no such merciful tendencies. Their AK47s chattered, sending flocks of slugs into the village indiscriminately to hit the thatched sides of houses. A couple of the running women were whipped to the ground in the hail of steel.

Falconi, infuriated, turned and rushed to the Frenchman. "Goddamnit! Tell your men to raise their fire till the women and kids are in the clear. We've got to give 'em enough time to reach that swamp."

Farouche defiantly cut loose with another burst of lowflying slugs. "Piss on the women!" he shouted. "If they live, they breed. And don't weep for the brats, *mon colonel*. Remember that nits grow up to be lice!"

Chief Brewster, staying a few paces to the rear, manned the Prick-Six radio. He took an incoming message, then yelled out to his commanding officer. "Skipper! Both Swift Elk and Mister Hawkins say the Meos are killing noncombatants."

Falconi reached out and grabbed Farouche's collar, almost yanking him off his feet. "You told us this would be a realistic test of your combat abilities. Shooting down women and children is not favorably impressive, Farouche!"

Farouche violently wrenched himself free. "This battle is not over yet, *mon colonel*! Perhaps there will be a surprise or two for you, eh?"

"Bullshit," Falconi said. He turned away in anger.

"Break off the attack!" the colonel bellowed. He motioned to Chief Brewster. "Pass the word!"

"Aye, aye, sir!" The Chief relayed the orders via the small radio.

"Are you mad?" Farouche asked. "We have a chance to wipe out these vermin. But we must move fast."

"You listen to me," Falconi said. "I don't care how goddamned dirty a war gets, neither my men nor I are going to kill those noncombatants in cold blood."

Farouche laughed crazily and pointed. "Look over there, *mon colonel*! In this war there are no such things as noncombatants. Only the living and the dead."

Falconi snapped his eyes in the direction indicated. He saw several young women, fully armed, returning fire from the questionable cover of one of the huts.

"Everyone fights out here, *mon colonel*," Farouche said laughing happily. "So we kill them all, eh?" He slipped a fresh magazine into his weapon, then aimed it at the women. Four quick pulls on the trigger blew them away like flowers in a hailstorm.

"Sonofabitch!" Falconi cursed in surprised anger.

"Skipper," the Chief said interrupting him. "You'd better take the radio. There's too much traffic for me to pass on."

Falconi grabbed the Prick-six. "This is Falcon. Over."

"Bravo," Swift Elk said identifying himself. "We're taking hits from outside the village. Over."

Falconi again turned on Farouche. "Now *we're* being attacked. What gives, Farouche?"

"You call me—"

"I'll call you a sonofabitch!" Falconi yelled. "What gives, goddamn you!"

Farouche grinned. "I told you this would be a test of combat skills to prove I deserve heavier weapons. Since you wanted to see my men and me in real combat where daring

121

and skill is needed, I have arranged exactly that. I have allowed us to walk into this. These bastards always have security detachments outside their garrisons and villages."

"You let us wander through them yesterday?" Falconi asked.

Farouche grinned and saluted. *"Mais oui, mon colonel!* And now you can see my men really fight."

"You're insane, Farouche! Fucking insane!" Falconi hollered in anger.

"I may be, but I can serve you well," Farouche insisted.

Falconi turned from him. He wasted no time in transmitting to his team leaders. "Alpha! Bravo! Move in to me. Over."

Neither Swift Elk nor Chris acknowledged receiving the message. They didn't have time. The gunfire built up as the enemy attack came in from the jungle. Falconi arranged the Command Element and the twenty Meos with them in a position to cover the two groups as they converged on the center.

In five minutes both team leaders came in from opposite directions. They ran like hell through the huts now smoldering from tracer rounds and the occasional grenades that had been tossed into them.

Chris was indignant as hell. "Where'd those bastards come from, sir? I thought all the enemy would be in the village."

Before Falconi could answer, a massed attack rolled in from the jungle. Every Black Eagle threw himself to the ground and delivered return fire. Momentum carried the front ranks of the enemy assault to within twenty meters before the effort came apart under the accurate fire.

Swift Elk made a quick assessment of the physical surroundings. "This fucking place is undefendable, sir," he said.

"Which leaves us with but one choice," Falconi said. "We'll have to leave."

"I couldn't have said it better," Swift Elk said.

Then an unexpected mass of fire came in from the jungle. A couple of Farouche's men crumpled to the ground as the others shot back in an attempt to force the enemy at least to withdraw a few meters back.

It didn't work.

"We're going to have to break out before we're completely surrounded," Falconi said. "The attackers are massing for a final assault on their own. Once they start, we won't be able to stop 'em."

"They are coming to rescue their families," Farouche said. "That makes them fierce fighters, *mon colonel*."

"Yeah," Falconi said, working the charging handle on his M16. "And makes our jobs twice as hard."

Farouche giggled insanely. "Too bad you didn't bring any mortars with you, *mon colonel*. We could blast their ranks into hunks of meat and stroll out of here in a style the befits true gentlemen."

"You and I are going to have a long talk after this," Falconi promised. "But in the meantime, would you mind preparing your men to support this movement?"

"There is nothing I have to do to accomplish that except yell, *'En avant,'*" Farouche said.

Falconi turned from him. He spoke to Archie, the Chief, and Frank. "Are you guys ready?"

"Let's do it!" Archie exclaimed.

"Black Eagles! Back into your original fire teams!" Falconi yelled at his detachment. "Alphas! Lay down fire with us. Bravos! Move forward toward the edge of the jungle!"

Chris, Paulo, and Hank had plenty of ammunition. With Paulo on full-auto, they cut loose into the enemy position. The Command Element joined them while Ray Swift Elk, Blue Richards, and Dwayne Simpson suddenly leaped to their feet and headed into the hell in the direct front.

123

They managed to get a good twenty meters distance, thanks to the covering fire. The team found good cover behind some fallen logs at the village edge. They dived into position and began laying down their own bullet-storm.

"Alphas!" Falconi yelled.

Chris and his men did exactly as the Bravos did. The combined fire of the other two teams and Farouche's Meos made the enemy duck their heads and return fire hesitantly. The Alphas passed the Bravos' position at the logs and dove to cover nearer the jungle's edge.

Falconi and his men were hot on their heels.

Farouche and his Meos caught on to the maneuver and carelessly joined in. By the time they joined the Black Eagles, there were ten of their number either lying in the stillness of death or writhing in agony between the new positions where they had begun the maneuver back in the village.

Now the small army was massed and there was nothing left to do but storm straight into the hell ahead of them. It was another all-or-nothing situation with but two widely diverse results possible:

Life or death.

Falconi took a deep breath. "Charge!"

Nobody noticed if their selector switches were on full or semiautomatic. They simply moved forward with rhythmic pumping of their trigger fingers. The steel-jackets swarms of bullets zapped into the enemy positions ahead of them.

The Meos, their natural lust for combat built up to uncontrollable heights, shrieked in their strange, high-pitched battle cries and ran wildly forward.

"Mes enfants!" Farouche yelled, trotting after them. "En avant! Soyez fier!"

The enemy ahead had entered the battle hastily and angrily. Practically unorganized, they were fighting as a mob of independent riflemen. Their fire was undirected and uncoordinated. Some, their own Meo instincts boiling through their psyches, leaped up and rushed toward Farouche's tribesmen. Their impetuosity cost them their lives as the Black Eagles' volleys blew them down in batches of five and six.

Within two minutes, both groups of Meos were entangled in shrieking, hacking, hand-to-hand combat. Bayonets, knives, and even Chinese swords slashed into flesh as they grappled in the jungle flora. Splatters of blood speckled the leaves of plants as the battle ebbed and swirled in the vegetation.

This new situation caused the Black Eagles' forward movement to hesitate, then cease. There was little fire coming at them. But Falconi knew it would be a certain death to remain in that spot, since Farouche's Meos were outnumbered. He had to get the momentum started again.

"Fix bayonets!" he ordered.

When the detachment was prepared, he motioned them forward with a wave of his arm. They slammed into the crowd of frenzied fighters, to begin their own slashing and stabbing.

Archie Dobbs forced himself into the melee and swung three hard, horizontal butt strokes that crashed into as many heads. He didn't know which tribesmen he was hitting, and he didn't give a damn. All the scout wanted to do was fight his way to freedom.

Swift Elk's own instincts had caused him to become as wild as the Meos. He was now a Sioux warrior, and like those noble plains fighters who had been born and bred for nothing but war and hunting, he went at it with his own voice screaming his people's most famous battle cry:

"Aiyeee! It is a good day to die!"

The Sioux counted coup with heavy slaps to enemy faces, then he drove his bayonet deep into the throat of one man who had leaped in front of him. Swift Elk quickly pulled the blade free in time to whirl and face another.

The individual, his eyes alight with dope and fighting

ardor, had abandoned his AK47 for the huge Chinese sword he held in both hands. Strung out or not, he was damned good with the weapon and fast as hell.

Swift Elk barely managed to sidestep a lightning-quick stroke of the big blade. The Sioux made a slashing attack with the bayonet, but hit only empty air.

The Meo attacked again. This time he was closer, and he took advantage of the distance. Two horizontal swings forced Swift Elk to stumble back and lose his balance, then another of those mighty overhead strokes whistled through the air toward the Sioux's head.

Swift Elk quickly threw up his M16 to block the attack. The thick blade bit deeply into plastic handguard. The Indian rapidly twisted his rifle and jerked the sword, still stuck in the M16, from the attacker's grasp.

The man wasn't about to let that stop his attack. He quickly dived on the Black Eagle and locked his hands around his throat. Swift Elk grabbed the man's wrists and bent back in a savagely quick counter-move. The Meo screamed as one wrist snapped under the pressure.

A sudden shot exploded nearby and the tribesman's head disintegrated as brains and goo blew all over Swift Elk's face.

Farouche laughed. "You are taking too long, Chief Sergeant." He reached down and grabbed Swift Elk's hands pulling him to his feet. Then the Frenchman pulled the sword from the M16 and handed the rifle to the Indian.

Swift Elk wiped at the crap that covered his features. A quick glance showed him that the detachment had moved forward almost twenty meters. He rushed toward them to catch up.

Farouche trotted beside him. "I came back for you, Chief Sergeant." He laughed. "You are as crazy as those Meos. You are a savage."

The enemy's will to fight was finally broken. The fighting died off as final shots were fired at the fleeing enemy

Meos. Falconi shouted, "Cease fire!"

Swift Elk and Farouche joined him. The others, Black Eagles and friendly Meos alike, now stood in silence. But they remained on the alert in case the enemy launched another unexpected attack.

Farouche made a quick check of his surviving men. There were damned few. He merely shrugged it off. "Ce'st la guerre. You want to go back to the village now, mon colonel? There would be a little more of a fight with the women, then we could have some fun raping them."

Falconi's face was streaked with sweat. "How soon before another enemy counterattack from a different source?"

"Twenty minutes," Farouche answered. "Maybe if we're lucky, a half hour."

"We're going back to Faroucheville," Falconi announced. He looked around for Archie and finally spotted him. "Take us home, Archie."

"Yes, sir!" the scout shouted back.

The column of Black Eagles and Meos formed up again. Farouche walked beside Falconi. "Can I have my supplies now?"

Falconi sighed. "Hell, yes! But we're going to have some long, hard conversation on tactics first."

"Get me what I want, mon colonel," Farouche promised. "And I'll do anything you ask."

Falconi said nothing as the small force moved deeper into the jungle for the downhill walk back to Faroucheville.

CHAPTER 13

Faroucheville was the picture of placid tranquility that particular evening. The night air outside was sweet with the fragrance of tropical flowers and a gentle, cooling breeze wafted through the village.

But the atmosphere inside Farouche's quarters was so thick it could have been cut with an M7 bayonet.

Falconi, Chris Hawkins, and Ray Swift Elk lounged in chairs while the Frenchman paced back and forth, chain-smoking his cigarettes with agitated motions. The man was angry, and his Gallic soul boiled with fury as he fought a strong natural tendency to fly into an uncontrollable rage.

Finally he turned and faced the Americans. "You are going too far! Too far!"

Falconi slowly lit his own smoke. The colonel didn't want to add fuel to the flame of Farouche's bad temper. It seemed that if he remained calm, the situation would not get out of control. But he had made a command decision and was determined to stick by it, despite the Frenchman's reaction.

Falconi took a deep drag, then lethargically exhaled. "Sorry, commandant. But we're soldiers. You must understand that."

"Of course, *mon colonel*," Farouche said. "I have been too long away from my own army, but I have not forgotten what is military discipline. But it seems you press me most unfairly."

"I work under strict guidelines," Falconi explained. "Unconventional warfare, while unpredictable and fluid by nature, still demands that certain standing operation procedures and regulations be observed." He shrugged. "So, as you can see, I have no choice."

"Of course, you have a choice!" Farouche snapped. "Who is here to watch you and direct you? Or to go so far as to press charges if they disagree with your decisions? Some general? A staff officer? There is nobody."

"I'm here," Chris said.

Farouche looked at him. "You mean to say that you would turn in your own colonel if he did not play exactly by the rules?"

"Sure," Chris lied. "I'm a soldier, too. My orders are—"

"I do not believe you!" Farouche yelled. "Do you think I am stupid? I know the loyalty you have for *monsieur le colonel*."

Swift Elk spoke up. "What about me?"

"You most of all would back him up," Farouche said. "A senior noncommissioned officer who turns against his commander is worse than a cobra." He lit a fresh cigarette off the dying embers of the old one. "You are ganging up on me. But I don't think it is because of your orders or the procedures dictated by your headquarters."

"What is your opinion of our attitude, commandant?" Falconi asked with sincere interest.

"That is easy to explain," Farouche said. "Look around you. What do you see? Nothing but wild, virgin country that is claimed by a nation that does not even have people in it. Perhaps your government desires to gain complete control of this domain, eh? Perhaps kick me out as well in the bargain. The international borders in this world mean absolutely nothing. It is the strong man who rules here."

"You mean like a warlord?" Falconi asked.

Farouche hesitated. Since he'd calmed down a bit, he

was now beginning to worry about completely losing control of his temper and giving away the true situation. "Perhaps that word 'warlord' is too strong, *mon colonel*. Instead, let us say 'partisan chief.' "

"I don't know about that," Falconi said. "There are enough men under your command to have conquered that village we fought in a couple of days ago. Why didn't you take along a sufficient force to get the job done?"

Farouche shrugged. "It didn't seem a tactically sound thing to do."

"Bullshit!" Falconi said.

"Do you call me *le menteur*—the liar?"

"Yes," Falconi answered.

"Me too," Swift Elk interjected.

"And I," Chris added.

Farouche trembled with rage for a few seconds, then the anger subsided. He tilted his head back and laughed. "You are trying to upset me. This is to test my personality under stress, *non*?"

"Certainly not, commandant," Falconi said. "We are not inclined to play silly psychological games when the present situation is so serious. My opinion of your actions is that you are unable to completely empty this village of fighting men because another group of Meos would attack and take Faroucheville while you were away."

"But *mon colonel*—"

"It would be like a leopard guarding a kill," Falconi continued. "When he sees a hyena nearing, he chases the one away. Yet another will sneak in and steal the meat."

"I have more control than that of this area," Farouche protested.

"I'm not stupid, Farouche! None of my men are," Falconi said. "It's easy as hell to see that there's some sort of power struggle going on in these mountains. I'm not sure exactly what type of situation we have here, but there're several groups pitted against yours and vice-versa. And this conflict does not smack completely of political or idealogical differences!"

Farouche, now thoroughly worried, gestured in a calming manner. "But, *mon colonel*—"

"At this point," Falconi continued, "the only thing I can figure out is that there is a territorial squabble here."

Farouche rubbed his hand across his mouth. He chose his words carefully. "*Mon colonel*, I have been out here for a long, long time. I have fought many years, and I do not deny that there has developed a certain amount of animosity between myself and other guerrilla chiefs. But, *mon colonel*, I am a loyal soldier of France. Those other sons of bitches change sides all the time. A certain group may fight the Communists with me. Then they are bribed to turn against me."

"That's a tough way to run a war," Swift Elk said.

"Of course, monsieur le sergent-chef," Farouche said seeking sympathy. "Who can I trust? Who is my friend? No one! And now you insist on making things difficult, too." He finished his cigarette and angrily threw it to the floor and stamped it hard with his heel. "*Bien!* I tell you what. I quit, eh? Exfiltrate me and I will pick up my back pay and spend it on Paris whores and cognac. There is nothing left for me."

"Don't be so fucking melodramatic," Falconi said.

"I am being realistic," Farouche insisted. "And after I spend the money, I will blow my brains out and that will be the end of it all. Because all these years of sacrifice and danger will have added up to *rien*—nothing!"

Now Falconi was beginning to think he'd gone too far. "Hold on, commandant. Let's make a deal. You're too valuable a man to be allowed to drop out of this struggle for freedom in Southeast Asia. Suppose I order in a supply drop of mortars, ammunition, and mine warfare equipment?"

"*C'est magnifique!*" Farouche exclaimed.

"What do we get in return?" Swift Elk asked.

"My friendship! My loyalty!" Farouche answered happily.

Now it was Falconi who chose his words very carefully. "I must insist on being in command." Before Farouche could protest, Falconi quickly continued. "It would still appear to your Meos that you are the commandant. You will give all the orders, and any meetings held between us would seem a staff conference between equals with you having the most influence."

"That is terribly unfair!" Farouche said.

"I really must insist," Falconi said. "My superiors expect me to maintain control and command while they pour weapons, ammo, and equipment in here. And I think that is reasonable, considering the high costs of such material."

"Mmmm," Farouche pondered. "And you would get me mortars and other heavy support armaments?"

"Yes," Falconi promised.

"Even plastic explosive?"

"You bet, commandant."

"In that case, *mon colonel*," Farouche said. "We have struck a bargain." He snapped to attention and saluted.

Falconi got to his feet and returned the gesture. "I am very happy that we have reached an amicable agreement, commandant. Believe me, it is really to your advantage."

Farouche nodded. "You are probably right, *mon colonel*."

"Now will you excuse us please, commandant? The detachment is having a party of sorts, and we're expected to attend."

"Of course, *mon colonel*," Farouche said. He walked to the door and opened it. "I will wait impatiently for the promised supplies."

"We'll order them in quickly. The drop can be made in two days," Falconi said. "Good day, commandant."

Farouche held the door as all three Americans left. He nodded polite good-byes, then eased the large portal shut. As he did so, Ming entered the quarters from an adjacent room. Farouche looked at him. "Did you hear it all?"

"They insulted you, commandant," Ming hissed in anger.

Farouche smiled easily. "*Ne traccasez pas*—don't worry. I shall have my revenge for their impudence."

"When will we kill them, commandant?"

"As quickly as possible after the supply drop," Farouche answered.

The phonograph was an old-fashioned type with a handle to wind it up. And the record on it was also far outdated. A nasal-voiced young oriental woman sung the song "China Night" in the Japanese language. Her high-pitched voice wavered and vibrated in the traditional style of Oriental singing:

"Shi-na no yoru, shi-na no yoru yoo-o-oh!"

The Black Eagles' hut was very dimly illuminated by a single lantern. Blue Richards, with both arms around a small Meo woman, swayed slowly in time with the music as they danced around the floor.

The other members of the detachment were with their own young women. Paulo Garcia and Dwayne Simpson finally took their new girlfriends and joined the dancing couple. Frank Matsamura, with a silly grin on his face, came in from a side door, his arm around a beautiful female companion of his own. They looked into each other's eyes, making it easy to tell they'd been doing more than just taking a stroll in the moonlight.

133

Only Archie Dobbs was alone. He sat on a stool in the corner, slowly tapping one foot in time with the music. He took a final sip from the bottle of Chinese beer he held. The detachment scout got to his feet and walked across the room to get a fresh bottle from a wooden box bearing oriental writing characters. He got a brew and laughed aloud.

Blue looked over the head of his sweetheart. "What's funny, Arch?"

"The beer's warm, but it ain't my fault this time," he said. "I'll bet there ain't a 'frigerator within a hunnerd miles o' this burg, huh?" He returned to his seat and sat down. He noticed a couple of the unattached females sitting on the other side of the room, but he made no move toward them.

Hank Valverde, sharing a beer with his own lovely companion, was puzzled. "How come you ain't made no moves on them other broads, Archie? They're ready, willing, and able."

"I agree," Archie said. "But I ain't messing with no female 'cept my Betty Lou."

"Aw, c'mon!" Hank scoffed. "You ain't turning down available pussy, are you?"

Archie took a hefty swallow of the warm beer. "Pussy don't mean nothing when you're truly in love."

Doc Robichaux looked over at Chief Brewster. "Has he always been like that?"

"Hell, no!" the Chief said with a laugh. "I ain't known him long, but he always struck me as one o' the horniest swabs I ever seen. And I been in the navy fifteen years."

"Gimme a break," Archie said. "I got high morals."

An explosive outbreak of laughter was choked off when Falconi, Swift Elk, and Chris Hawkins stepped into the hut. The colonel grinned. "What's so funny?"

"Archie don't want no pussy, sir," Paulo Garcia explained.

Swift Elk looked at his friend. "What's the matter, Archie. Did your dick fall off?"

"Goddamnit!" Archie swore. "You guys really make me sick, you know that? You're a bunch o' damn rutting animals. I swear to Christ you got your brains in the heads o' your peckers, 'cause that's what you seem to think with."

"Just don't turn into a preacher-man, Archie," Blue begged of him.

"Then don't try to get me to do something I don't wanna do, okay?"

"I got something more serious to talk about," Hank Valverde said. He left his woman and approached Falconi. "Sir, we got a favor to ask. The guys is really got some sweet setups for shacking up. We're wondering if we can get our own hootches. All the women are willing to move in with us."

Falconi jerked a thumb toward Swift Elk. "That's up to the top sergeant here."

Swift Elk surveyed the scene. Every man had a woman, and he could tell he'd have his own pick from the ones left over. "It's okay by me, but I don't want you guys scattered all over the village. Set up housekeeping, if you must, but do it close to this hut. There's still guard duty and a few other soldiering details to tend to."

"Thank you for bringin' me down to earth," Blue Richards said. "For a minute there I thought I'd died and went to heaven."

Swift Elk didn't smile. "You're still in the armed forces, Blue."

"That's something I'll never forget with you around," Blue said.

Swift Elk checked his watch. "As a matter of fact, first relief is due on post in fifteen minutes."

"Okay! Okay!" Doc Robichaux said. He bent close to his girlfriend's ear and whispered in it, then turned to Dwayne Simpson. "C'mon. Let's get that two-hour stint over with so we can get back to more pleasurable pastimes."

"Right on!" Dwayne said.

Falconi helped himself to the beer. "You guys invited me to a brew, so I'll have it now. Then I'm off to my own affairs."

"Hey, sir!" Archie called out. "We've seen her!"

"Give me a break," Falconi said. But he couldn't suppress a grin. He tipped his head back and chug-a-lugged the entire bottle. When he finished, he gasped. "This stuff is awful!"

"Right, sir," Blue said. "Watch this." He went to his corner of the hutch and returned with his M16 rifle. He aimed it at Hank Valverde. "Drink a bottle o' that beer or I'll blow your ass to kingdom come."

Hank feigned fear. "Okay, Blue, don't shoot!" He obediently picked up a bottle and quickly drank it.

Blue handed the rifle over to him. "Okay, Hank. Now you make *me* drink a bottle."

Falconi laughed and shook his head at the staged joke. "I'm leaving you crazy bastards before I go as nuts as you."

"See you later, sir," Paulo Garcia said.

"Kiss her for me, sir," Archie sang out.

Falconi waved and stepped out of the hut. He walked a few yards down the village street to his own quarters. He could see the faint lantern light coming from the window.

Sari, kneeling on a rice mat on the floor, looked up when he entered. She displayed a sweet smile. "I have been waiting for you, Robert."

"And I've been thinking about you all day," Falconi said. He stripped off his clothes to begin what had developed into a custom between them.

Sari also went to the buff. Together they walked to the corner, where a rustic bathing area was situated. It was no more than a drain hole in the floor beside a tub of water. Sari dipped a gourd ladle into the cool liquid and poured it

136

over him. After he was soaking wet, she picked up a bar of soap and began lathering him down.

Falconi sighed in contentment as her small hands gave him a quick, sensuous massage as she washed him clean. "Robert, you must speak to me while I bathe you," Sari said. "You cannot stand there like a mute."

"Is that a Meo custom?" he asked.

"Yes," Sari answered. "When a woman washes her warrior, he tells her of his day and what the morrow brings for him."

"There's not much to tell," Falconi said. "I can't remember anything, anyway."

"Then I will ask you questions," Sari said working the suds from his chest down to his crotch. "Then we will go to the bed and you will have your way with me, as befits a noble fighting man."

Falconi looked at her. "If you Meos start up your own army, let me know. I'll sign up for a ten-year hitch."

"You see?" Sari said. "There are many enjoyable customs when you are with my people." She pushed her lithe body against his, the soap slippery on their flesh. "Now we must talk and deepen our man-woman friendship before physical pleasure."

Falconi smiled lethargically. He could feel her firm nipples and soft breasts against his belly. "Sari," he sighed. "Ask me anything. Anything!"

CHAPTER 14

The conditions were ideal for a supply drop. There was only a bit of a breeze, and it was blowing in the direction of the flight. The drop zone was the same one used by the Black Eagles during their infiltration into the operational area. It was long, wide, flat, and soft.

A small group of people gathered around the panels that would be used by the aircraft crew to spot the correct place on the ground to dump their valuable cargo via parachute. They would also use it to determine which direction flight the DZ control officer had determined to be the best.

Lt. Col. Robert Falconi, Sgt. Archie Dobbs and Chief PO Leland Brewster, represented the American detachment. Lucien Farouche, his chief lieutenant, Ming, and a working party of a dozen Meos were also in attendance round the DZ marker.

A total of three brightly colored panels had been laid out in the form of "T" on the ground. The plan was to have the aircraft fly in direction of the "stem" of the letter, and drop its cargo on Falconi's verbal command via radio.

Farouche fidgeted with impatience, his eyes scanning the skies for the first glimpse of the airplane. He glanced over at Falconi. "Do you really think they will deliver everything you have requested, *mon colonel*?"

"It's all been confirmed, commandant," Falconi replied. Farouche was like a kid at Christmastime. "Don't worry.

The full complement is on its way. I've been assured of that."

"Sixty-millimeter mortars and machine guns, eh?" Farouche asked for the tenth time that day.

"And ammo and plastic explosives," Falconi added. "The complete load is on its way."

"After all this time it seems too good to be true," Farouche said. "I have been operating short of proper supplies for nearly fifteen years."

"This is easier than looting it off dead enemy troops or raiding a depot for it," Falconi said. He nudged the Chief, who squatted by the radio. "Get a confirmation on the ETA."

"Aye, aye, sir," Chief Brewster said. He pressed the transmit button on the communications gear set up in front of him. "Fly Guy, this is Falcon. Over."

After only a couple of seconds of waiting, the speaker crackled. "This is Fly Guy. Over."

"Request another Echo-Tango-Alpha," the Chief said. "Over."

"Roger, Falcon. Wait." There was a pause of a half-minute. Then the air force man returned on the air. "Echo-Tango-Alpha in two-one minutes. Over."

"Roger, out," Chief said. He looked at Farouche. "Twenty-one minutes to go, commandant. They'll also raise us again for a final confirmation on the azimuth. The colonel will be in control at that point."

"Thank you," Farouche said politely. He lit a cigarette and smoked intently, as he always did when he was anxious or angry. "I will be glad when this is over."

Archie lit up his own smoke. "We do this all the time. It's pretty routine for us, commandant."

Farouche shook his head. "There is no such thing as routine in this part of the world, Archie Dobbs. There is a vast no-man's land outside of the villages and hamlets. This is a wilderness where tigers, cobras, and armed men prowl."

"We have security out," Archie reminded him. "Both our fire teams and a bunch of your Meos got the area pretty well wrapped up. We got surefire protection. Frankly, I don't think even a slithery-assed cobra could get in without one of our guys noticing it."

"I don't wish to be disagreeable," Farouche countered. "But there is nothing 'surefire' in an operational area like this one. And I should know. I was stranded out here through bad luck and misadventure."

Before Archie could make any further remarks, the radio came to life again with the voice of the aircraft's pilot. "Falcon. This is Fly Guy. Over."

Falconi took the microphone from the Chief. "This is Falcon. Over."

"We are making the final turn. Request the azimuth. Over."

"Roger, Fly Guy," Falconi answered. "Make approach on Two-Five-Niner. Over."

"Roger. Two-Five-Niner." Then the pilot issued the security challenge. "Request confirmation. Over."

"Roger," Falconi said back. "Read for confirmation. Over."

"This is Fly Guy. One-Zero-One. I say again. One-Zero-One. Over."

"Fly Guy, this is Falcon," Falconi said into the microphone. He paused as his mind quickly calculated. Then he spoke again. "One-Four-Eight. I say again One-Four-Eight."

The security confirmation had been a simple one. The pilot spoke a number, and Falconi replied with one that would add up to 249 when placed with the pilot's. This was a preselected sum that was in the classified portion of the OPORD.

"Confirmation, accepted, Falcon," The pilot replied. "We are turning in for the run. Echo-Tango-Alpha in three minutes. Over."

"Roger, We are ready. Wait."

Falconi's senses, as were everyone else's, were fine-tuned for both the sight and sound of the aircraft. Finally he could hear it. Then the aircraft, a C-130 flying at a bit under one thousand feet, came into view. Falconi waited until the plane cleared the trees and was over the drop zone.

"Execute! Execute! Execute!" he exclaimed tersely into the microphone.

A series of bundles suddenly appeared out the open rear doors of the big transport. Immediately bright-colored parachute canopies blossomed forth, and the equipment eased toward the ground in wide oscillations. These particular chutes were designed specifically for equipment drops. Not having to be concerned with frail human cargo with arms, legs, and necks to break, their designers had made their rate of descent much more rapid than normal personnel parachutes.

Farouche, excited, let out a cheer. *"Sacre!"* At last the big stuff is here! *Vivent les americains!"* His Meos followed his example, uttering their shrill shouts, as was their custom.

At the same time a sudden outbreak of gunfire exploded on the north side of the drop zone.

Now Ray Swift Elk's voice was on the air. "This is Bravo. We've just been hit by a force estimated to be five-zero to six-zero enemy. Over."

"Bravo, hold 'em there till we get the goodies off the Delta Zulu," Falconi said.

Farouche had already sprung into action. he yelled and gestured at his Meos. *"Vite! Vite! Saisez l'equipment! Allez au village!"*

Then a fresher and louder burst of spewing weaponry broke out on the west side of the drop zone. Chris Hawkins, situated in that area, came on the air. "Falcon,

141

this is Alpha. Unknown number of enemy have attacked our position. Over."

"Goddamnit!" Falconi swore. "They're directly between us and the village."

"We'll have to fight our way through 'em," Archie said. He'd pulled his M16 off his shoulder and cranked the charging handle. "Ol' Farouche was right. There ain't nothing but nasty surprises out here."

Farouche had only one thing on his mind at that point. He wanted to get the new equipment out of danger as quickly as possible. He ran among his Meo porters kicking and punching them, punctuating each blow with curses and threats. "Move faster, you lazy bastards!" he bellowed. "If I lose as much as one mortar round or a single block of plastic explosive I'll shoot the lot of you! *Pressez-vous!*"

The little, stocky Meos reacted quickly. They tied the heavy bundles to the long wooden poles they had brought with them. Then, in teams of two, they hefted the loads to their shoulders and began to trot off the drop zone.

Several fusillades of bullets slapped the air over their heads. The Meos instinctively ducked and moved faster. But the following volleys came in lower. Cries of anger, fear, and pain sounded in the gunfire, and several loads hit the earth as the carriers themselves were mowed down.

Falconi immediately summed up the situation and reacted quickly and correctly. "Bravo, this is Falconi. Move back onto the Delta-Zulu and cover the withdrawal of the working party. Out!"

Swift Elk heard the broadcast orders. He didn't bother to acknowledge them. Instead he yelled out to his team. "Pull back! We gotta cover the carrying detail on the drop zone! Let's go."

Although the three riflemen in the team were relatively new as a team, their reaction was swift. Blue Richards, Dwayne Simpson, and Doc Robichaux went to full-auto,

142

kicking out a curtain of steel that blew away the front rank of the attackers who had begun to press in on them.

This created a brief lull in the fighting. The Bravos took advantage of this temporary relief to break contact and haul ass. They ran through the jungle and burst out in time to see the porters being mowed down as they struggled with their heavy burdens.

"Enemy left front," Swift Elk yelled.

Blue, Dwayne, and Doc quickly turned the muzzles of their M16 rifles in that direction and cut loose. Their fire was effective enough to allow the surviving members of the carrying party to gather up the loads of their dead and wounded comrades and begin the dangerous toil of getting the gear off the drop zone.

But there was still the large force engaging the Alpha Fire Team to be dealt with. And they were strongly positioned on the most direct route back to Faroucheville.

Farouche had gathered his remaining force—a group of fifty Meos—and ordered them forward toward the enemy.

Falconi, who had been returning fire from the prone position, leaped up and ran toward the Frenchman. He flung himself to the ground before him. "Wait, commandant!"

Farouche's face displayed an expression of puzzled anger. "*Attendre*—wait? What for, *mon colonel*? We must attack immediately to break through the force between us and the village."

"That will cost us too many casualties," Falconi said. "A frontal assault is definitely not the way to go." He interrupted his argument to cut loose with a couple of fire bursts toward a particularly annoying portion of the enemy line.

"We cannot go around them," Farouche said. "It will take too long because of the heavy loads. We will only find ourselves in this same predicament at another location."

"Goddamnit!" Falconi hissed angrily. "We've got heavy

143

weapons in those bundles, Farouche. There're six beautiful 60-millimeter mortars, complete with ammunition. Hell, we can blow the bastards to pieces and waltz back to the village, for Chrissake!"

But Farouche shook his head. "No, *mon colonel*! I will not waste the ammunition."

"Jesus Christ!" Falconi yelled. "You're trading your men's lives for mortar shells!"

"*Exactement, mon colonel*," Farouche said with a grimace. Then, before Falconi could stop him, he leaped to his feet and shouted assault orders to his men. "*En avante! A l'attaque!*"

The Meo force scrambled to its collective feet and surged forward. The Black Eagles had no choice but to follow.

There was absolutely no finesse in Farouche's attack. His men simply stormed the enemy positions in the surrounding jungle. The men in the front of the assault melted away in the defensive fire coming in at them from the bad guys. Despite these heavy losses, their comrades in the back pressed forward, leaping over their fallen tribesmen.

The explosive rattle of small arms fire built up into a deafening crescendo to the point that it drowned out the enraged bellows of the combatants as well as the screams of the wounded and dying.

At one point the assault faltered and even the stubborn savagery of the Frenchman's Meos did not help. They took a sudden influx of incoming fire, and the quickly escalating number of losses broke up their attack.

Swift Elk, with his Bravos, was in front of the Black Eagle detachment. He quickly read the situation and ordered Blue, Dwayne, and Doc forward on full-auto. Then he turned and motioned to Chris Hawkins.

"We gotta shore 'em up at this point, Chris!" Swift Elk yelled. "Send your guys in with mine."

"Roger, Ray," Chris shouted back. It made no difference at that point whether he outranked the Sioux Indian or not. A quick battlefield decision had been made, and Chris elected not only to follow it, but to lead his own men in behind Ray Swift Elk.

Paulo Garcia was in the middle of the Alpha fire line. Hank Valverde covered the left flank, and Frank Matsamura performed the honors on the right. They were able to move faster than the Bravos and caught up with them within a couple of minutes.

There was a wall of Meos ahead of them. The little men, fighting wildly and unwisely, were still sustaining losses at an alarming rate. There was a definite, immediate need of disciplined fire power.

The Black Eagles provided it.

Now seven abreast, with Swift Elk in command slightly to the rear, both teams entered the fray. Well-aimed semiauto shots zapped into the enemy area as both Paulo Garcia and Blue Richards fired overlapping patterns of full automatic bursts of 5.56 millimeter volleys.

The Command Element arrived and joined the skirmish line. Falconi and Chief Brewster "dressed right" on the others as riflemen, but Archie Dobbs's battle fever had gotten to a high pitch. He surged forward with the Meos, firing in a wide semicircle into the enemy positions.

The enemy incoming rounds subsided slightly, then were cut down by a half.

The combinations Black Eagle/Meo attack continued to move forward, picking up speed in the same relation that the bad guys' shooting was dying off.

Then it was all over.

It dawned on everyone that there was no one in front of them. Even Archie Dobbs turned around and walked back to join his buddies. He found Falconi. "The way is cleared back to the village, sir."

"Right, Archie," Falconi acknowledged. He signaled to his team leaders. "Form in column. Alphas right, Bravos left." He looked around for Farouche until he sighted him.

"Bring those porters up here and put 'em in between my teams."

"Of course, *mon colonel*!" Farouche happily replied. "The supplies are safe, *n'est pas*? All intact, eh?"

"Maybe so," Falconi said wearily. "I wish I could say the same about my sanity."

Farouche walked up to the American. "Are you troubled about something, *mon colonel*?"

"Would you be surprised if I were?"

Farouche looked defiantly into the American officer's eyes. "Sometimes you seem a worrier to me, *mon colonel*."

Falconi sighed. "Commandant Farouche, you and I are going to have to have another long heart-to-heart talk."

CHAPTER 15

This time it was Falconi's turn to be angry and for Farouche to be on the defensive.

The occasion was another meeting in the Frenchman's quarters. Farouche sat in his favorite chair and nursed his customary scotch and soda between drags of one of the American cigarettes that Falconi had provided for him.

Farouche had patiently listened to Falconi's ass-chewing for a bit more than a quarter of an hour. But he didn't feel the slightest anger or resentment. In fact, he was close to giggling in delight. The arrival of six 60-millimeter mortars, two hundred rounds of ammunition, thirty pounds of C4 plastic explosive, a dozen M79 grenade launchers, eight M60 machine guns, and other miscellaneous equipment and munitions had put him in a downright jolly mood.

"Please, *mon colonel*," he said in a soothing voice. "Be forgiving of me, eh? My life has been tragically difficult these past fifteen years. I have been here for so long with so little that perhaps I have developed what you consider bad habits."

"Bad habits?" Falconi fumed. He sat across from Farouche with Ray Swift Elk and Chris Hawkins standing behind him. The colonel leaned forward, his eyes boring into the Frenchman. "There's more here than just bad habits!"

"I don't understand your problem," Farouche said. "In fact, I think you are a bit overemotional about something that is not all that serious."

Falconi forced himself to calm down. "Let's not argue, commandant. Instead, allow me to ask some questions. All right?"

"*C'est bien,*" Farouche agreed.

"Who attacked us on the drop zone?"

"Communist partisans," Farouche answered.

"Bullshit!" Falconi snapped.

"Mmmf!" Farouche snorted. "Who do you think it was, eh? Maybe the Nazi army?" He pointed at Swift Elk. "Or a tribe of American Red Indians, *n'est pas?*"

"Listen to me, Farouche," Falconi said. "This isn't my first war. I've been in every kind of combat there is outside of a nuclear holocaust. I've been locked in conventional land battles and prowled jungles as a guerrilla. But I've never seen the likes of this local situation."

"What is so different here?" Farouche asked. "Except we are so far from any major population or military centers? After all, we are but a rather primitive combat zone."

"Hell, this *isn't* a combat zone," Falconi said. "It's like a series of feudal fiefdoms. We hit a village here and there, and they hit us. But there's no coordinated action against us. No counterinsurgency troops move in and sweep the area. There are no unfriendly aircraft flying reconnaissance missions trying to locate our main camp. There's just a bunch of independent actions that don't accomplish shit, except to reduce the local population."

Farouche shrugged as he got up to mix another drink. He turned from his liquor cabinet. "Are you sure you don't want one?"

"Positive," Falconi said.

"What about you two?" he asked Chris and Swift Elk. When they also refused, he fixed another scotch and returned to his chair. "I don't understand your confusion, *mon colonel.* This is partisan warfare peculiar to northern Indochina."

"No, it's not," Falconi countered. "This situation smacks of gang warfare."

Farouche nervously wiped at his mouth. "*Absurdité!* I have explained that these other groups are partisans and militia who change sides all the time."

"How can they change sides?" Falconi asked. "There's no one up here, except the North Vietnamese army. And the Red Chinese are farther north. These locals can't jump back and forth between the ARVNs and NVAs."

"Do not forget, *mon colonel*! I am here," Farouche said in a hurt tone. "A representative of the *république français*—a soldier of freedom, eh? What about that?"

"So what are you offering these others that make them make switches—albeit temporary ones—to the western cause?" Falconi inquired.

Farouche thought fast. "Well—er, that is easy to answer, *mon colonel*."

"So answer me!"

Farouche took a deep breath. "I—uh, I promise them things from the West. Like money and other rewards." He took a deep drink. "That is it! Of course, these are empty offerings, because I really have nothing. And, naturally, when I fail to deliver they turn against me and rejoin the Communist cause."

"Why tell them you can give them things that you can't possibly deliver to them?" Falconi asked.

"*Bien*, it is because I am desperate," Farouche explained lamely. "I must do something!"

Falconi abruptly changed the subject. "Why didn't you use those mortars this morning?"

"I didn't want to waste the ammunition," Farouche said. "I told you that during the fighting."

"I can get you more shells," Falconi said. "You know that."

Farouche decided to display a great deal of moral indignation. He leaped to his feet. "I make my decisions as

149

commandant! Must I explain each and every one I arrive at during the heat of battle?"

Falconi frowned. "You goddamned bet your ass you do! We made an agreement that in reality I was in command."

"Must I constantly remind you I am a soldier of France? That gives me certain rights to alter any agreements when I think it is necessary."

"The hell it does! And I want to know who attacked us on the DZ, Farouche," Falconi said, standing up. "I won't buy any shit about them being a Communist force." Falcon realized he was losing control of his temper. "Never mind answering now. We'll talk tomorrow." He walked to the door with Swift Elk and Hawkins following. "We're going to get this all cleared up before we go out on ops again. And I'm not kidding!"

Farouche watched the trio of Americans leave. He sipped his drink and smiled coldly. "Ming!"

Ming stepped into the room. "Yes, commandant."

"I wish to speak with Sari."

"She is outside, commandant. I will fetch her immediately." The Meo quickly left.

Farouche had time to freshen his drink and light another cigarette before his chief lieutenant arrived with the girl. He turned and held his arms outstretched. "Come to me, *ma pigeon.*"

Sari happily raced across the room and allowed him to embrace her in his muscular arms. She snuggled her head into his chest. "Oh, *mon amour! Chéri!* How I have missed you!"

"And I've missed you, too," Farouche said. He leaned down and kissed her hard, brutally on the mouth. Then he abruptly pushed her back and held her shoulders tightly in his meaty fists. "What have you learned from Falconi?"

"*Rien*—nothing," Sari said. "The man will not talk."

Farouche's eyes narrowed in anger. "You slept with him like I told you, *non?*"

Sari lowered her gaze. "Yes."

"You gave yourself to him as a woman?"

Sari sighed. "I did everything you told me. I allowed him to take my body." She looked up into his face. "But he could never have taken my heart."

"To hell with your heart, bitch!" Farouche snapped. "You were supposed to get information from him."

"I'm sorry," Sari cried. "I tried—"

Farouche slapped her hard on the mouth. "You are a cunning, lying bitch!"

Sari wiped at the trickle of blood that seeped from her lips. She sobbed. "There was nothing more I could do."

"You were supposed to be intimate with him," Farouche said. "I expected him to look upon you as a trusted confidante." He turned and walked away from the young woman. "Bah! You are no good even as a whore! You stupid, useless tart!"

"Robert Falconi would not speak to me of military matters," Sari protested. "No matter how I tried to turn the conversation, he would change it back to other things." She began crying harder. "It was—so difficult for me— *mon amour*—to let another man have his way with my body—I tried so hard for you—please believe me, *chéri!*"

"Did he not even give a hint about anything?" Farouche demanded to know. "What does he think of me? How long does he plan to stay here? Will he bring in more supplies?"

"I know nothing," Sari said helplessly.

Farouche stared furiously at her. "You don't like another man to touch you, eh?"

Sari shook her head. "I hate it, *chéri!*"

"How would you like to find yourself with many men?" he asked heartlessly. "Perhaps if I threw you to some of my roughest men for their enjoyment you would try harder with Falconi. Or perhaps I shall pass you over to Wang Fu's gang. Those bastards would love to have a little playmate like you. You might even last three or four days

151

with them."

Sari's horror was reflected in her eyes. "You wouldn't do that to me, *mon amour*. You say you love me."

"Get me a drink, you little bitch!"

"Oh, don't call me insulting names, *chéri*," Sari begged. "I cannot bear it!"

Farouche grabbed her by the hair and propelled her toward the liquor cabinet. His fury showed clearly in his loud voice. *"I said fix me another drink, you shitty bitch!"*

Her feelings shattered by the callous insults, Sari walked across the room to tend to the task. She wiped at the tears that ran down her face as she poured out the scotch into a fresh tumbler.

Farouche turned his attention to Ming. "Falconi must die now. And that means all his men, too."

Ming wasn't convinced. "Perhaps we should try to get some more supplies first."

Farouche shook his head. "It is too late. Falconi is in no mood to request more weaponry and equipment from his superiors. He is already extremely suspicious of the situation here. I had enough trouble passing off not using the mortar shells during the fighting on the drop zone. I could not tell him I wasn't sure he would be alive later to get more for me. And, I fear, it is only a matter of days before he finds out he and his command have been inserted into the middle of an opium war."

"It won't be easy to kill the Black Eagles, commandant," Ming warned him. "These are seasoned fighters, and pretty tough fellows."

Sari handed Farouche his drink, then walked over to one of the chairs and sat down. She knew better than to make a lot of noise, so she quietly wiped her tears while the two men conspired against their American guests.

Farouche sipped the scotch. "I have an idea, Ming."

Ming smiled. "You are going to employ trickery, commandant?"

"Of course. The problem will be to get them all together in once place at the same time," Farouche said. "I think we shall have a banquet." He smiled without humor. "Of course, since the Black Eagles are our guests of honor, they will be seated at a table by themselves."

"That will make them a convenient target," Ming suggested.

"Of course," Farouche said. "We will have this gala affair in the large communal hut." He laughed. "It would certainly add insult to injury, if the killing was done by a couple of the machine guns that Falconi requested for us."

"Yes, it would," Ming agreed. "We could hide them outside, with the muzzles of the weapons aimed through the thatched wall at the Black Eagles."

Farouche nodded. "At a nod from me, you are to tip off the gunners and they will fire two entire belts of ammo into the *merdes*, eh?"

Ming was thoughtful for a few moments. "Some of our people have developed a fondness for these Americans, commandant. They might become upset if they are killed."

Farouche shrugged. "We will explain that Falconi and his detachment were about to betray us. That should satisfy most of the complainers." He paused. "Of course, we will have to shoot the rest that don't believe us."

"Of course, commandant," Ming coldly agreed.

Farouche walked over to Sari and roughly jerked her from the chair. "And as for you, bitch! Get back into Falconi's bed. You fuck him, suck him, or whatever it takes. But find out what is going on between him and his headquarters. After he dies I must know how to handle his superiors' inquiries."

Sari swallowed hard. "Yes—yes, *mon amour*."

"And, remember! If you fail me, there'll be more than one man that will know your body. How would you like me to sell you to one of the Red Chinese army squads we deal with, eh? Those fellows would screw you to death within

153

seventy-two hours."

"You wouldn't do that!"

Farouche slapped her hard. "You can depend on it, bitch!"

Archie Dobbs threaded his way across the dark hut between the swaying couples dancing to "China Night" playing on the old Victrola. The Black Eagles had scoured Faroucheville in the wild hope of turning up a different phonograph record, but had been unable to locate another. They decided having but one song to dance to wasn't so bad in the light of having so many lovely and willing females around.

Archie fetched himself another beer and opened the bottle. He squatted down on the floor to enjoy the brew and to watch his Black Eagles pals waltzing and romancing the local ladies. Now and then one of the guys would take his woman and leave the party for a while. They would return happier and more placid to resume dancing.

Archie sensed that someone had walked up beside him. He glanced up and noticed one of the Meo girls standing beside him. "Hi," he said pleasantly.

"Hello," she said. She sat down on the floor beside him. "You are called Archie?"

"That's me," Archie replied with a grin. "What's your name?"

"Lina," she answered. "You do not have a woman, Archie?"

"Not here," Archie said. "But I got one, you can believe that."

Lina slipped her arm around him and placed her head on his shoulder. "Don't you need a woman here?"

Archie felt the passion soar up in his gut, but he fought it down. That was one hell of a good-looking broad hanging on to him. "I made a promise to my lady."

154

Lina reached out and gently massaged a very sensitive spot on him. "I will be your lady."

Archie endured it for as long as he could, then he gently removed her hand. "Lemme explain something, Lina. Me and my Betty Lou made a bargain. I don't screw nobody else and she don't either."

"She is your wife?"

"Naw. Nothing like that," Archie said. "We ain't even talking marriage or nothing. But we made a commitment to each other, see?" He knew that the girl was from a society where sex was something that was to be enjoyed without a lot of complicated entanglements. But he was trying to make her understand.

"How long has it been since you've seen your woman?" Lina asked.

"A couple of months," Archie answered.

The girl's eyes widened in surprise. "You have not been with a woman in all that time?"

"Nope," Archie stood up quickly. "And if I don't take a walk right now, that particular record is gonna fall hard."

"Where do you go, Archie?" Lina asked.

"Outside, baby," he answered. Archie left her and hurried through the door. He paused long enough to take another look at his buddies, then at Lina, who was now on her hands and knees looking up at him in puzzled amusement. Her breasts were easily visible through the top of her dress neckline.

Archie quickly turned and walked rapidly away. "Holy Toledo!" he hissed to himself. "It's hell being a saint!"

CHAPTER 16

It is not unusual for a person to take abuse from another. There are generally good reasons—at least to the person taking all the crap—to put up with it. But, as a wise man once said, there are limits to practically everything.

Rebellion, whether it be a revolution against an indigenous, oppressive government or resistance to a cruel occupying military force, begins with the utterance of but one single word. It is a simple one, but the most powerful in any human language. That word is:

No!

And that was what Sari finally said to Farouche's heavy-handed, disrespectful treatment toward her. Sari said "No!" Pride, self-worth, and anger played a big part of it as she followed the usual pattern of rebellion. That next step—the one that took her past the point of no return—was:

ACTION!

The beautiful young Meo woman waited patiently for Lt. Col. Robert Falconi to return to his quarters from his duties. When he finally arrived, she met him at the door and took his hand. After leading him across the room to the best chair in the hut, she sat him down and served him a cup of hot Chinese tea. Then she knelt in front of him.

"Robert," Sari said softly. "I have important information for you."

Falconi took a drink of the green liquid. From the serious expression on the woman's beautiful face, he sensed that something important was in the air. "I am listening, Sari."

"Robert, Commandant Farouche has lied to you," she began.

Falconi shrugged and laughed. "I figured that out a couple of weeks ago. Can you be a bit more specific?"

"He has told you that he is fighting Communist forces but that is not true," Sari said. "He is fighting other warlords."

Falconi sat the now empty cup on the floor and lit a cigarette. "I had begun to think I was in the middle of some sort of power struggle," he said. "Is he trying to gain political control of this area?"

"Not political control," Sari said. "This is the opium country. He wants to own all the poppy fields in these mountains."

"Opium?"

"Yes, Robert. I think you have not seen the bricks. They are black and hard, this size." She held her hands out to indicate the dimensions.

"Wait a minute! That sounds like the dehydrated rations that were picked up on that ambush," Falconi said. "Archie Dobbs saw some of those and told me about them."

"That was dried opium," Sari said. "Ready for market and worth much money."

"That clever sonofabitch!" Falconi exclaimed. "But who does he sell the narcotics to?"

"They are taken north to Red China," Sari explained. "The government there buys the goods for shipment to the West."

"God! I hate to say it, but it's damned near poetic justice. Those bastards are getting sweet revenge for the

157

opium trade forced on them by western nations in the last century," Falconi said. "And by poisoning our youth at the same time, they figure they're adding to the decadence of the West."

"The Chinese buy from Commandant Farouche and the other warlords," Sari continued. "They pay in American dollars and French francs. All cash."

"That goddamned Farouche has a sweet setup here," Falconi said. "What the hell did he want us in here for?"

"He needs big guns to slay his competitors," Sari said.

"Yeah," Falconi said. "Mortars and heavy machine guns would give him a distinct advantage in these constant skirmishes." He thought a minute. "But why couldn't he get them from the Chinese? He's gotten light arms from them."

"They will not supply such weapons to any of the warlords," Sari said. "It is to their advantage to have them fighting each other. It keeps the price down when there are many. If one of them got big guns, he could destroy the others. It would create a king with much power."

"It'd be quite a monopoly, and the winner would sure as hell raise his prices," Falconi said. "So asshole Farouche gets on a radio and starts broadcasting his old G.M.I. codes and gives us a song-and-dance about fighting Reds for fifteen years. He says he needs heavy weaponry to carry on the war. And we believed him."

"But he didn't want them to send anyone here to help him," Sari said. "He was very angry when he learned you and your men were coming."

"I'll bet that bastard was!" Falconi said. "So since we're here, what're his plans?"

"Oh, Robert! He is going to kill you all. There will be a feast to honor you, but he will have the fast-shooting guns hidden to murder you and all your brave men."

"A feast? When?"

"I think within a week," Sari said. "Perhaps three or

158

four days from now. I am not sure."

Falconi was silent for a while. "So why are you telling me this, Sari?"

She cast her eyes downward in shame. "He has used me as a whore with you, Robert. I was to spy on you. But when I had no information to give him, he was cruel and said he would give me to another gang of opium sellers. He even said he might let Chinese soldiers have me." She looked up, tears welling out of her eyes. "He said he loved me, Robert. And I believed him and loved him, too."

"I'm truly sorry for you, Sari." Falconi said.

"You have been kind to me, Robert, and gentle, too. I think I am beginning to love you now," Sari said.

Falconi left the chair and knelt beside her. He kissed the girl gently. "I appreciate what you've done, Sari. You have put yourself in danger, but I will figure a way to get out of this without showing you warned me. Don't worry."

"If you escape, I will die happy," Sari said.

"You won't die," Falconi promised her. His expression turned grim. "But I won't say the same for Farouche, and he sure as hell won't check out of this world on any glad notes!"

Swift Elk and Hank Valverde made a careful examination of the new equipment. The Sioux top sergeant called out each item and the number on hand as Hank duly noted the totals in his supply accounts book.

"Okay," Swift Elk said. "We got twenty-two bandoleers of 5.56 ammo here."

"Roger," Hank said, checking off the number. "Twenty-two bandoleers."

Swift Elk went to another crate and opened it. "And here we got—"

"Hey, Ray!" Archie Dobbs stepped inside the hut. "The Falcon wants to see you right now."

"Yeah, Archie," Swift Elk said. "I'll be finished in—"

"He means like this fucking minute, and he ain't kidding," Archie said. "When the Falcon says 'immediately if not sooner,' he means exactly that."

"Sounds serious," Swift Elk said. "Take a break, Hank. I'll be right back. He left the supply sergeant and followed Archie down the village street to Falconi's quarters. When he got there he found Chris Hawkins also waiting.

"Gather in close," Falconi told him. "I have some rather important intelligence to pass out to you."

Archie, Swift Elk, and Chris pulled up chairs close to their commander. Falconi began calmly and completely to disclose all the information that Sari had passed on to him. It took a full quarter of an hour before all questions had been asked and the situation was fully understood.

This was followed by a couple of beats of stunned silence.

Then Swift Elk asked the most obvious question. "What's the exfiltration plan?"

"That, top sergeant, is exactly what this meeting is about," Falconi said. "There's no doubt we've got to get the hell out of here. We could never overpower Farouche and all his men."

Archie Dobbs licked his lips. "Damn, sir! You're talking about us traveling out of Laos all the way through North Vietnam to reach our own lines in the south. That's about—"

"Here's a map," Falconi said. "Check it out."

Archie pulled his plastic G.I. map scale from his pocket and quickly figured the distance in question. He whistled in amazement. "Man! That's seven hundred fifty kilometers!"

Chris Hawkins preferred mileage when discussing trips. "That's damned near five hundred miles."

"And every inch of the way unfriendly and dangerous," Swift Elk added.

"We ain't got any maps available of the area south of here," Archie said. "And I know for a fact that there ain't none to steal in this village, neither. We'll be moving in the blind with nothing but a compass and wild-ass hope!"

Falconi smiled at his scout. "Well, Archie, I think this will be the challenge of your career."

"If you consider traveling through nearly half a thousand miles of trackless, improperly mapped country filled with ornery bastards who would like to kill us, a challenge," Archie said calmly, "then I suppose it is."

"I like your sense of perspective, Archie," Chris said. "You are completely and totally insane."

Archie grinned. "How else could I stand you bastards?"

"Okay," Falconi said. "Now that we've examined the humorous side of this thing, I'll issue a quick, verbal OPORD. The first task to perform is to inform the men, and impress them with the need to remain normal and not cause Farouche or his Meos to think we suspect anything."

"No problem," Swift Elk said. "The guys are pros."

"Right," Falconi agreed. "The next thing is to get ourselves equipped for the trip. That means we'll steal back some of the goodies just dropped in."

"What about what's left over?" Archie asked.

"Blue Richards can give a practical demonstration of his skills with C4 plastic explosive by blowing it to hell," Falconi said. "Which will have to be timed to go off a few hours after we've vacated the premises."

"Blue can handle that," Swift Elk said. "He's damned near as good as Calvin Culpepper."

"I wish Calvin wasn't on administrative furlough with Malpractice," Falconi said. "But, like you said, Blue can do the job. The one thing I want impressed on him is to make sure none of that stuff is blown into the areas where the noncombatants live."

"That means the fighting men in there with them won't be hit either," Chris reminded him. "They'll survive to come after us. We're already badly outnumbered as it is."

Falconi shook his head. "I don't kill women and kids!"

"No matter what we do," Swift Elk said. "We're going to have to get our timing down exact. A missed maneuver or forgotten detail can lead to our massacre."

"Too bad we can't rehearse the operation. And I have another question," Archie said. "Do we let SOG know?"

Falconi shook his head. "We can't take that chance. Farouche managed to broadcast out of here all the way to Saigon. There's no assurance that he isn't monitoring the airways to check on our radio traffic."

"Hell, sir!" Archie reminded him. "He don't know our codes."

"No," Falconi agreed. "But he knows enough about military commo to figure out a different sort of message has gone out rather than a normal report or supply requisition. If he suspects anything in the slightest, we've had it."

"This," said Chris uttering one of his calm New England understatements, "is a sensitive situation."

"I'll tell you something," Archie added. "While we're stealing stuff to take with us, there's something else we ought to grab ahold of, too."

"What's that?" Falconi asked.

"Some of that bastard Frenchman's scotch," Archie said. "I need a drink—bad!"

"Bullshit," Falconi countered him. "We've got to keep our heads clear for immediate action." He looked over at Swift Elk. "Top sergeant, it's up to you to keep the guys cold sober and ready to move."

Swift Elk nodded. "Yes, sir. As sober as proverbial judges."

Archie frowned. "That's a hell of a way to run a railroad!"

Farouche strolled through the village with a jaunty stride. He whistled a bright tune and winked at Ming, who accompanied him. When they reached the Black Eagles' hut, they stopped and rapped on the doorpost.

Blue Richards sauntered over. He nodded a greeting. "Howdy."

"Howdy!" Farouche said, imitating him. "And how are my American friends?"

"Fair to middlin'," Blue said. "Ya'll c'mon in and sit a spell."

Farouche stepped inside. Ming followed, grinning, his head bobbing up and down in pseudo-friendliness. The Frenchman held his arms wide open and beamed at the eight Americans sitting there. "Ah, *mes camarades-aux-armes!* It is so good to see you." He looked around. "But where is the brave colonel and his master sergeant?"

Chris Hawkins, lounging in a hammock hanging in one corner of the room, looked over lethargically. "I think they're making up a duty roster or something. Is there something important?"

"Of course!" Farouche said. "We are going to have a party!"

"Wow!" Blue Richards said.

Frank Matsamura, who was cleaning his M16, stopped his work. "Can we bring our women?"

"Oh, I'm sorry," Farouche said. "It is a Meo custom that such feasts be attended by the men only."

Doc Robichaux was not pleased. "Sounds shitty."

"You must not refuse," Farouche told them. "The Meo men are having this to honor you, their brothers in battle. Afterward, you can practically consider yourselves members of the tribe. Like me."

Chris sat up in the hammock. "I'm sure Falconi will not refuse to attend."

"Of course not," Farouche said. "Monsieur le colonel has the best manners, eh?"

"So, as second-in-command, I accept for everyone," Chris said. "We will be all there. Thank you so much for asking."

"You are welcome, monsieur le lieutenant," Farouche said. "It is tomorrow evening."

"Tomorrow?" Chris asked.

"Yes," Farouche said. "A surprise, *non*?"

"A surprise, yes."

"It will be most enjoyable," Farouche said. "A special evening, believe me. He and Ming waved exaggerated and friendly good-byes, then left.

Blue walked across the room to Chris. He leaned down and spoke in a whisper. "That means we move tonight."

Chris stood up. "I'll let the Falcon know."

"This is some dangerous shit!" Blue complained.

Archie Dobbs only grinned. "What's that the Falcon is always saying?"

"You mean, 'Nobody said this job was going to be easy'?" Chris asked.

"That's it!" Archie exclaimed.

"Yeah, Archie," Blue agreed. "But nobody said we was goin' to be left high and dry up here at the Chinese border all on our own, either."

Archie laughed. "Hell, Blue! Why do you think Uncle Sam issued you such a damned good pair o' boots, huh?"

Blue was not in a good mood. "Maybe to die in."

CHAPTER 17

Blue Richards and Frank Matsamura, their M16 rifles slung over their shoulders, sauntered back and forth on their sentry post. A Meo tribesman, pulling the same duty, leaned against a tree next to the supply hut and watched the casual, soft-spoken pair with a disinterested gaze.

The two Black Eagles continued to chat quietly together as if nothing particularly special was on their minds. But beneath their cool exteriors, they felt a great deal of apprehension. Despite this appearance of indifference, they were involved in a quickly planned, highly organized and coordinated escape and evasion scheme that Robert Falconi had desperately conceived within the course of a half hour.

This dangerous situation had been unexpectedly thrust upon the detachment with Commandant Farouche's announcement of the party to be thrown in their honor the next night. Sari's warning that the affair would be a cover for their massacre necessitated the perilous haste.

Now it was close to midnight and Faroucheville was quiet. But for the previous four hours the entire Black Eagle Detachment had been deeply involved in preparation for their escape from the village. It was going to be damned difficult to pull off. They had to avoid arousing suspicion, yet be able to knock off their usual routine of casual beer drinking, dancing, and fornicating with their Meo women.

At the same time, there were countless tasks to be attended to.

This delicate situation had been handled outwardly by Swift Elk while Falconi and Chris Hawkins did the more clandestine tasks. The Sioux top sergeant had feigned being angry with the men over their sloppy attendance to duties. That afternoon he had given them a good ass-chewing and told them that all equipment would be checked out in no less than a full field inspection.

Farouche's chief lieutenant, Ming, had gotten word of the activity and passed it on to the Frenchman. Farouche, mildly curious, had left his quarters to see what was going on with his American guests. What he had found was feverish activity in preparation for the inspection. He noted Swift Elk severely supervising the work. The Frenchman approached him politely and respectfully. "What is going on, monsieur le sergent-chef? Are you displeased with your men?"

"I sure as hell am," Swift Elk snapped. "These sons of bitches have really been getting careless lately. The only thing they've got on their minds is beer and pussy."

Farouche laughed. "It is the same in *toutes les armes*—all the armies. When the situation gets out of hand it is up to the senior noncommissioned officers to put it right."

"That is absolutely correct," Swift Elk agreed. "And I'll tell you something else. I sent the women away for tonight. A long, sexless night ought to teach those horny fuckups to keep their minds on straightening up their act and keeping it that way!"

Farouche was immediately suspicious. Without the women around, the Americans would be able to do things unobserved. "Is monsieur le colonel going to set an example by sending the woman Sari back to her family's house?"

"Hell, no!" Swift Elk said. "A colonel don't have to do what enlisted snuffies do. You don't think I'm gonna pull

166

a full-field on him, do you?"

"Of course not," Farouche said, feeling relieved. If all the women, particularly his spy, had been evacuated from the Black Eagle area, he would have suspected they knew of the plot to kill them the next night. "I think you are correct, monsieur le sergent chef. A time without the comfort of *l'amour* will make your soldiers change their ways, no doubt," he agreed.

The Frenchman stuck around for another fifteen minutes out of curiosity about U.S. military methods. What he saw was every man's gear, including weapon and a full load of ammunition, laid out per SOP. Extra clothing, boots, rations, *et al* were gathered together in the proper manner.

"Some o' the guys are even losing stuff," Swift Elk said. "We're going to make up shortages now, and the careless bastards are going to sign Statements of Charges."

"Statement of Charges?" Farouche asked. "What is that?"

"It is a military document in which they are charged with the cost of lost and missing items of equipment," Swift Elk explained. "The money is taken out of their pay."

"Ah!" Farouche exclaimed. "That is what is called a *Document de Responsibilité* in the French army." He watched a bit more. "Well, monsieur le sergent-chef, I wish you good luck in your efforts." He had walked away chuckling to himself as he thought how handy if would be to find the Americans' property gathered so neatly together after they'd been massacred the next evening.

This work had continued, with Swift Elk's voice, loud and angry, promising more severe punishment if things weren't put right quickly and permanently.

But by early evening, the pseudo-inspection had accomplished exactly what was intended by it all along: Every man-jack was packed and prepared to move out at a moment's notice.

Now Blue and Frank continued their slow sentry stroll, edging closer and closer to the unsuspecting Meo guard by the supply hut. Frank fished a cigarette out of his jacket pocket. "Got a light, Blue?"

"Nope," Blue answered. "You know all I do is chaw, Frank."

"Yeah. I forgot." Frank gestured to the Meo. "Got a match, buddy?" He walked up to him, pointing to the end of his cigarette.

Surprisingly, instead of a match, the Meo fished out a rather solid-looking Chinese cigarette lighter. He was able to flick it only once.

Frank brought the heel of his hand up in a quick uppercut and put the guy's lights out. The Meo stumbled back into Blue's arms. Blue gently lowered him to the earth. At the same time, Frank pulled some parachute suspension line from under his pistol belt and began tying the guy up.

"Where're we gonna leave him, Frank?" Blue asked.

"Let's put him in the shack," Frank suggested as he finished binding up the guy.

"Hell, let's toss him into the jungle over there," Blue countered. "I don't like the idea of putting somebody next to a charge and having him go up with it."

"Suit yourself, pal," Frank said. "Just remember. If he survives, he'll be one of the bastards chasing us in about twelve hours."

"I'll kill in combat," Blue said. "But I won't blow up a defenseless man. I ain't a murderer."

The two picked the Meo up and carried him into the jungle. As a final precaution, Frank took out a hypodermic that Doc Robichaux had prepared. He administered the dose of morphine to make sure the guy slept soundly.

Then Frank stood by the door of the supply hut while Blue went inside. Blue pulled the timer mechanism from his ammo pouches and quickly assembled it in the illumination of the small penlight he'd brought with him. Afterward, he went to the crate of C4 and prepared a shaped charge out of a quarter-pound block of white plastic. Falconi had given him definite orders to make sure there would be no harm to the part of the village where the noncombatants lived. The only thing the explosion was to accomplish was to destroy the mortars, machine guns, and other equipment brought in on the supply drop.

Blue worked quickly and efficiently. He situated the shape so that it would blow outward away from the village. After capping and fusing the charge, he set the timer to electrically detonate the explosive in four hours.

The Alabaman went outside. "Okay, Frank. Let's go."

Robert Falconi packed up the last of his gear, then returned to Sari who sat on his bed under the mosquito netting. "We owe you a lot."

Sari ignored the expression of gratitude. "I want to go with you," she said.

Falconi shook his head. "I'm sorry."

"I will not be a burden, Robert," she said. "I was born and raised in these mountains. I have been on many journeys through them."

"I'm sure you have," Falconi said. "But there will be much fighting and—" He hesitated. "I'm afraid our chances are not very good, Sari. We must travel by foot through many miles of enemy-held territory. I cannot even arrange a pick-up by aircraft. There is no available landing zone that is safe enough. My men and I must walk all the way back to South Vietnam."

"I am not afraid!"

"Of course you're not," Falconi said. "But I'm afraid for you. Believe me, you'll stand a better chance with Farouche even than with us."

"There is a secret way out of the mountains into a valley

169

that leads to the south," Sari said. "It has been used for generations in the smuggling of opium. If you used that route, you would make it safely for certain."

"Do you know where it is?" Falconi asked.

"Not exactly," Sari admitted. "But there is a thick stand of jungle trees and bushes at the entrance. Perhaps I could help you find it."

"It's too risky," Falconi said.

"What do you plan to do with me?"

"We'll tie you up and give you shot of one of Doc Robichaux's drugs," Falconi said. "By the time you wake up, we'll be gone and Farouche will find you unconscious. I'm sure he'll believe you knew nothing about this."

Sari sighed. "I must tell you something, Robert."

"Yes?"

"It is something I have discovered about myself," Sari said. "I denied it to my heart, but since you are leaving soon, I can no longer smother the emotions. In these past few hours I have realized how very strong it is within me. I must let you know."

Falconi feared she had witheld information from him when she'd informed on Farouche. "What is it, Sari?"

"I love you, Robert." Her voice was soft and pained.

Falconi was touched by the sincere sentiment. He tried to reply in as kind a way as he could. "In my way—a soldier's way—I love you too, Sari," he said. "Do you understand what I'm saying?"

"Yes, of course. I understand you do not want a wife," she said. "Or at least you do not want me for one." Then she raised her lovely, almond-shaped eyes to his. "Or do you already have a woman?"

Falconi smiled. "No, Sari. There is no one." He thought of Andrea Thuy, the only woman he could ever love, who was away in America making a new life for herself after several harrowing episodes with the Black Eagles. He smothered the memories that pained him. Falconi glanced up and noticed that Doc Robichaux had quietly eased himself into the hut.

Doc raise the hyperdermic in his hand to signal that it was ready.

Falconi turned his gaze back to Sari. He smiled fondly at her, then swung his fist around sharply and slugged her hard on the jaw. The small woman spun completely around under the impact, and the American caught her in his arms. He picked her up and laid her on the bed.

Doc hurried across the room and pulled Sari's arm out straight. It only took him a few seconds to find a vein and deftly insert the needle into it. After working the plunger, he pulled the instrument free.

"How long will she sleep?" Falconi asked.

"Five or six hours," Doc answered. "You want to tie her up, sir?"

"Yeah," Falconi said. "We've got to make it appear that she was roughed up."

"You did that all right," Doc remarked, noting the blood in one corner of her mouth. Like Frank Matsamura, he had some parachute cord off the cargo chutes. He used it to tie her to the bed. Then he pulled a G.I. sling out of his medical kit to use as a gag.

"Do you think we'll need that?" Falconi asked.

"Not really," Doc answered. "That was a pretty strong shot I gave her." He paused. "On second thought, she could choke on it."

"Forget the gag, then."

"Yes, sir," Doc said. "See you later, sir, I've got to get back to my team."

"Tell the guys I'll be there shortly," Falconi said. As Doc left the hut, he looked down on the Meo woman. Her eyes were closed as her mind sank deeper and deeper into the gentle morphine sleep. Falconi leaned over and kissed her lips, tasting the saltiness of her blood. Then he checked the parachute cord to make sure it was tight enough to be convincing, but did not hurt her.

"Good-bye, Sari," he whispered. "My life as a professional soldier is made up of memories that run the gamut from violent and wicked to sweet and sentimental. If I survive to old age, I'll still remember you as one of the best."

He pulled his gear from under the bed and put it all on. Pistol belt, harness, bandoleer, grenades, buttpack—everything. Then he grabbed the M16, already locked and loaded, and headed for the door. He stopped at the exit and looked back at the woman now visible on the bed in the soft moonlight streaming in through the windows.

"Maybe, Sari," he said to her. "I would have learned to love you, too."

Then the Falcon went outside to go to war.

Archie Dobbs, at the head of the small column, was itching for action. He and Chief Brewster waited for Falconi to join them.

Archie nodded to his commander. "Ready to roll, sir?"

"Yeah," Falconi answered. He looked at the navy chief. "How's the commo gear?"

"All destroyed, sir," the Chief said. "The main stuff was to damned heavy to carry on an escape-and-evasion operation. Nobody'll ever use it again."

"What about team commo?"

"We got them reliable Prick-Sixes, sir," the Chief answered.

"Okay," Falconi said.

Frank Matsamura appeared out of the darkness. "Chris said I was to report to you, sir."

"Right," Falconi said. "You'll be sticking with Archie until we've cleared Faroucheville. After that rejoin the Alphas."

"Yes, sir."

"Falconi took a deep breath and slapped Archie on the shoulder. "Well."

"Well, what, sir?"

"Let's go."

Archie, with Frank behind him, turned and led the way on the route he'd chosen through the village. They passed the supply hut and silently entered the woods, walking softly past the Meo sentry who, like Sari, snoozed away the night under the influences of Doc's drug supply.

Finally Dwayne Simpson, the last man in the column, left the village limits and followed the penetration into the jungle.

The Escape-and-Evasion into five hundred miles of enemy-held territory was underway.

CHAPTER 18

The timing device that Blue Richards had set slowly ticked through its syncopated mechanical routine until the sear holding the trigger snapped back and cleared the way for the striker to slam shut on the electric connector. At that exact second, as the sun announced its impending arrival for the day with a few pink rays on the far horizon, the explosives in the supply hut detonated.

The monstrous clap of thunder shook the village huts so hard that dust, insects—and a couple of snakes—fell from the thatched ceilings. One carelessly constructed habitat collapsed altogether on its lazy resident, engulfing the unfortunate along with his wife and six children in a stinging pile of dried palm fronds and wooden slats.

Lucien Farouche, through sheer instinct, leaped from his bed and was half dressed before he was fully awake. The girl beside him was barely aware that something had happened as the Frenchman grabbed the M16 that Colonel Falconi had provided him. After picking up a bandoleer of ammunition to complement the rifle, the Frenchman rushed outside.

In the streets a stunned, confused populace was waiting for some sort of direction or orders. However, as per regulations and drill imposed long before by Farouche, the fighting men had rushed off to their predesignated defense firing posts, the shrill cries of subordinate leaders urging them on. They flung themselves into their fighting holes on the edge of the hamlet in anticipation of an imminent attack from rival opium gangsters.

But there was nothing but silence.

After ten minutes had passed, Ming sought out and found his chief. "Commandant! Commandant!" he cried.

Farouche, in his dug-in command post in the village center, came out. "Ming! Over here!"

"The supply hut is destroyed, commandant," Ming said. "Except for the personal M16 rifles that were issued out, everything we received on the supply parachute drop is destroyed. There is not a machine gun or mortar left."

"Sacre nom de nom!" Farouche bellowed in rage. He glanced around. "Are the Americans on the perimeter?"

"No, commandant," Ming answered. "They are gone."

"Partis—gone?"

"Yes, commandant," Ming said. "I went to their quarters and no one was there. Then I searched out several of their women. They said the master sergeant made them go away last night to punish the men."

"I know that," Farouche said. "I talked with monsieur le sergent-chef about that late yesterday afternoon. Perhaps he made them camp outside the village." He was suddenly very suspicious. "Let us go to Falconi's hut. If he is with his men, Sari can tell us what happened."

The people had recovered somewhat from the surprise of the explosion. With no more disturbance or even gunshots, they had settled down to wait. Farouche and Ming dispatched messengers to assure them that everything was under control.

The Frenchman charged into Falconi's quarters and went directly to the bed. He ripped the mosquito covers aside, then stopped in stunned surprise at the sight of Sari, bound tightly, sleeping peacefully. He slapped her face hard several times. "Sari! Sari! *Eveillez-toi*—awake!"

The woman did nothing but sleep on.

Ming leaned over Farouche's shoulder. "Look at her mouth, commandant. She has been struck a hard blow. There is smeared, dried blood there."

Farouche grabbed her shoulders and shook her hard. "I said wake up, you bitch!"

Ming, calmer than his boss, reached out and pulled one of her eyes open. He noted the dilation of the pupil. "She is drugged, commandant."

Farouche dropped her back to the bed. "Let us go to the supply hut."

When they arrived at the site, they found nothing but scorched earth. There was no hole, not even a slight depression, but it appeared as if the building had been swept away by a giant, burning wind.

"This was not an accidental explosion," Farouche said with professional appraisal. "A very talented and skilled *destructeur* has worked his craft here."

Ming walked out into the nearby jungle searching for pieces of equipment. All he found were useless scraps and bits. Then he stopped.

"Commandant! Come here."

"Eh? *Que voulez-vous?*"

"I have found one of our guards, commandant," Ming said. "Like the woman, he is tied and drugged."

Farouche joined his chief lieutenant and examined the unconscious man. Then he glanced back at the former site of the supplies. "These were blown up in such a way as to cause the force of the explosion to go outside the village, Ming."

Ming nodded in agreement. "Yes, commandant. If the blast had gone the other way it would have killed a lot of people."

Farouche laughed. "Yes! A lot of noncombatants would have been wiped out. That is something monsieur le colonel finds most offensive."

"Yes, commandant," Ming said. "Do you think he truly

caused this explosion?"

"Of course!"

"But if he spared women and children, he also spared the fighting men who lived and slept among them. If he has fled, that will mean a large force can follow him."

"In the end," Farouche said, "that will prove the undoing of Falconi. He will destroy himself and his men by his own stupid kindness."

"Shall we mount an immediate pursuit, commandant?"

"Form a tracking patrol to see if a trail can be discovered," Farouche said. "In the meantime, we must try to wake Sari and question her. There is a chance she may know enough to help us."

"Where would Falconi and his men hope to go?" Ming asked.

Farouche shrugged. "I admire their courage, Ming. But they are in the midst of the opium cartel. If they manage to get through that, there is an entire Communist army between them and safety."

"We can have them in our own hands within twenty-four hours," Ming said, hurrying off. "I will organize a tracking team to begin our pursuit."

Murphy's Law states that if there is any possibility of something going wrong, it most certainly will do exactly that.

Archie Dobbs's Law states that if there are any coincidental incidents in a combat situation, they will most certainly not be in the Black Eagles' favor.

The detachment had been on the move for five solid hours through the mountainous jungle. Four of those had been in almost complete darkness, with Archie's uncanny sense of direction taking them along the correct southerly compass azimuth. The going had been difficult and slow, but because of there being no necessity for backtracking,

177

Falconi and his men had made remarkable distance under even those difficult circumstances. After the sun came up, the trek became much easier and the pace was stepped up.

Things looked good—damned good.

But, coincidentally, coming straight at them from the opposite direction, was a large force of opium gangsters under the command of an ethnic Chinese warlord by the name of Wang Fu.

Wang Fu and his men were the recipients of the raid on the village a couple of weeks previous by the Black Eagles and Farouche's Meos. They had been mauled and humiliated. Now, heavily armed and strongly motivated, they were looking for revenge.

Their objective that particular day was Faroucheville. The ardor for combat and revenge had made them careless as they had traveled through the mountains the previous day. They had camped that night with a near maniacal desire to do battle, but the distance—though damned loud—explosion at dawn had sobered them up some.

Neither Wang Fu nor his men knew what the source of the detonation was, but it had brought them into a slightly more logical frame of mind.

Now they approached the coming battle with no less determination, but a hell of a lot more common sense. Their scout, who had been leading the rush pell-mell toward Faroucheville, had slowed down considerably. He now moved cautiously and alertly, holding his AK47 at the ready as he closely examined the path he'd chosen to follow. His senses were alert, and his eyes and ears were taking in all sights and sounds in the wild environment.

And he sighted Archie Dobbs before Archie saw him.

The AK47 round cracked at the same instant that Archie's eyes swung back to sight the Meo. Luckily, the bullet zapped through empty air and the Black Eagle scout was able to get off a snap shot.

The quick reaction caused the enemy point man instinctively to duck at the same time that he cut loose with another round. This one was wilder than the first.

By that time Archie had flung himself down and squeezed off two shots.

They missed, but Paulo Garcia had rushed forward at the sound of the shooting. The marine brought his rifle up and fired twice. Both rounds punched home, flinging the Meo off the trail into the bushes.

The remaining force of opium gangsters charged forward at what they first perceived to be some of their old rivals in the narcotics game. In cases like this, it was generally the first charge that won the day.

But the Black Eagles had a fighting style of their own.

When the first shots were exchanged between Archie and the Meo scout, Paulo had gone forward as per operating procedure. Hank Valverde and Frank Matsamura, Paulo's teammates in the Alphas, each took a separate side of the trail.

Chris Hawkins, as team leader, immediately alerted Falconi back in the middle of the formation of the situation that was fast unfolding at the head of the column.

Now, covering each other, Archie and Paulo moved backward to link up with the rest of the Black Eagles. Meanwhile the Command Element and Fire Team Bravo took up defensive firing positions along both sides of the trail.

All this happened within a matter of ten seconds—just enough time for the attacking Meos, screaming and bellowing in rage at the tops of their voices, to sweep into the impromptu ambush.

Well-aimed and -directed M16 fire from the Black Eagles swept up and down the line of attackers. Caught virtually flat-footed, the raiders were quickly slowed in their running assault, then brought to a standstill as their first casualties pitched to the ground in crumpled heaps. Confused and infuriated, the survivors attempted to return

179

fire, but in their hasty confusion were unable to lay down any accurate salvos.

The final volleys of M16 fire slammed them down like spinning, screaming bowling pins. Only a few lucky ones in the rear were able to back out of the hell zone and stumble to the rear.

They bumped into their leader, who was moving toward the fighting with the remainder of his forces. Wang Fu was clearly disturbed by the sight of the dazed survivors. "Why do you flee, cowardly dogs!" he screamed at them.

One of the men fell to his knees and beseeched his chief. "There are thousands up there, Honorable Wang! It must be the same army that attacked our village!"

Wang kicked him hard, knocking him to the ground. "Am I a leader of sniveling children or of fighting men?" He turned and beckoned to the others. "Follow me! We will deal with these louts of the French pig, then Faroucheville and its loot and women will be ours."

His Meos cheered and hurried after their chief. Wang rang crashing through the brush brandishing his AK47 over his head. He regulated his pace so his men could pass him up. Only when an informal vanguard was formed did he increase his gait.

But suddenly he stopped amidst an unexpected outburst of incoming small-arms fire. The men in front of him melted away in the hail of bullets. Wang Fu wisely turned and stopped his other men pressing in behind him.

"Move back! Move back!" he ordered in a shrill voice. "There is, indeed, an army facing us!"

The opium gang turned as one man and fled wildly through the jungle, leaving the scene eerily quiet, except for the groaning of the now deserted wounded.

Archie Dobbs and Paulo Garcia stepped back on the trail. Archie turned the selector on his rifle back to semiautomatic. "That's a good sex lesson for them bastards," he said.

"Sex lesson?" Paulo queried. "What the hell are you talking about—*sex* lesson?"

"We taught them bastards not to fuck with us," Archie said.

Sari's head ached from the drug that had been pumped into her via the hypodermic, and her mouth was sore from the hard punch that Falconi had given her. She sipped the hot tea as she sat on the edge of the bed.

Farouche stood in front of the woman. "Well?"

Sari raised her eyes. "What is it you wish to know, *chéri*?" She was careful to continue using terms of endearment with him to avoid suspicion.

"Don't be so stupid!" Farouche said. "I want to know what went on during the last hours that Falconi was here."

Sari took another sip of tea. "He was suddenly acting very suspicious, *chéri*," she said. "I began to suspect something unusual was about to happen. I tried to warn you, but he would not let me leave here."

"Mmmm," Farouche nodded. "Did he tie you up then?"

"No," Sari answered. "But when I told him I wanted to visit my parents' home, he forbade me to go. I asked him why, and he said—" she lowered her head to feign shame— "he said that he would want my body and to wait until he was ready."

"And you didn't try to run away?" Farouche asked.

"You told me to please him, *mon amour*."

Farouche didn't like being put on the defensive even that slight amount. He scowled as he spoke. "But what was going on that made you think something unusual was about to happen?"

"Oh, *chéri*, there was much coming and going here," Sari said. "His men would come in and talk in whispers. Finally, I insisted that I must see my family. It seemed most important to alert you. The last thing I remembered was that he struck me hard." She gently rubbed her sore mouth. "And then nothing."

"You are such a stupid little bitch!" Farouche said. He was so angry he wanted to hit her himself, but he calmed down and sighed in resignation. "I suppose there was really nothing more you could do under the circumstances."

He was interrupted from further comments when Ming suddenly entered the hut. "A messenger is here from Wang Fu."

"Wang Fu?" Farouche asked in disgust. "What does that piece of shit want?"

"He has had a battle with a group of white men," Ming said. "He is calling for a meeting with all the opium warlords. He thinks the situation calls for our groups to band together."

"For once I agree with him," Farouche said. "It is the only way to handle monsieur le colonel and his men. Tell Wang Fu I will be there. But find out where and when."

"It will be this afternoon at the Ghost Tree," Ming said. He referred to a spot where local superstition held that the spirits of dead Meo chiefs and wise men dwelled.

"A logical spot," Farouche said laughing. "Soon there will be another leader's ghost living in that *sacre* tree—that of Monsieur le Colonel Robert Falconi!"

CHAPTER 19

The religion of the Meo people was one fraught with taboos, superstitions, and spirits. They used these beliefs to explain the unexplainable, to understand the mysterious, and to bear up under the misfortunes and misadventures that befell them during their relatively short lives. Though these beliefs were not particularly deep or intellectually stimulating, they helped the people endure their hard existence.

There was a certain unique tree high in the opium mountains that would have attracted attention to itself under any circumstances. It was a huge broadleaf evergreen, a species common to the region, but this particular one was an ancient giant that had long ago choked out any plant competitors for food in the soil and sunlight in the sky. Its mighty trunk supported a height of sixty feet, sending its heavy branches cascading out over a broad area. This blocked out light penetration to the forest floor, thus leaving a large, naturally clear area around its base.

Over countless generations a legend had developed around this tree. The Meos believed that it attracted the spirits of their dead leaders and shamans, thus providing a habitat for wisdom and guidance. For this reason, it was known to all the Meo tribes as the Ghost Tree.

It was taboo to live near the Ghost Tree, and no warfare or squabbles were permitted in the vicinity in the belief

that a lingering, horrible death would overtake any tres-
passers or despoilers of this sacred area.

The only activity permitted beneath the Ghost Tree's
great foliage were meetings and councils between the various peoples to reach solutions to perplexing problems. It
was believed that the wisdom of the dead ancients would
influence the decisions reached there, thus benefitting
those concerned.

Now a group of men had gathered there for just that
purpose. These were opium warlords called there by one of
their number to deal with the sudden appearance of a
deadly fighting force in their midst. The man who had
sumoned his enemies to deal with this common nemesis
was Wang Fu.

The others present were Xan Tiu, Phong Lee, and
Lucien Farouche. Each warlord, with three of his closest
men situated to his rear, sat in a loose circle. They waited
for Wang Fu to address them.

Several women were present. They served a ceremonial
tea and bowls of rice to show the dead spirits present that
the gathering was done in peace. After this symbolic meal
was eaten, Wang Fu rose up.

"Greetings, brothers," he said executing a polite bow.
After each had bent down to touch his foreheads to the
ground to indicate their respect to him, he began his
speech.

"Several weeks ago one of the villages of my growers was
attacked at dawn," Wang Fu said. "Many people died
there and the village was left in ruins. When I was first
informed of this unfortunate event I presumed that one of
you brethren had led this attack." He paused and glanced
up into the branches of Ghost Tree to attract the spirits
there. "And I forgive you now for any trespasses against
my people."

Lucien Farouche grinned to himself, but imitated the
others by holding out his hands in a gesture of accepting

the forgiveness.

"I visited the village and heard a disturbing report from the survivors," Wang Fu said. "They said there had been Europeans among those who attacked them. These white men were described as fierce fighters."

Xan Tiu, a warlord with a nasty cut scar running diagonally across his face, spoke up. "Were these white men a large group?"

"Yes," Wang Fu said. "There were hundreds of them."

Again Farouche hid his amusement. But the remaining warlord, Phong Lee, was skeptical. "How could there be that many of them, Brother Wang? It does not seem possible!"

"But it is true, Brother Phong," Wang insisted. "For yesterday I myself was involved in a big battle with them."

Farouche was interested. "Where was this, Brother Wang?"

"In the south valley, Brother Phap," Wang answered. He used the Vietnamese word for "French," as did all the others when addressing Farouche.

The Frenchman was amazed the Black Eagles had managed to get that far. "Did they do you much harm, Brother Wang?"

Wang rolled his eyes in a gesture of agony and despair. "It was horrible, Brother Phap. They attacked us by the hundreds, killing my men as if they were slaughtering water buffalo for a great feast."

Xan looked meaningfully at Farouche. "What do you know of these racial kinsmen of yours, Brother Phap?"

Farouche paused, knowing that to be caught in a lie would mean his death after the meeting. He spoke carefully. "I know of these Europeans because they came here to seek me out."

"Are they French?" Wang asked.

Farouche shook his head. "No. They are *My*—American."

185

There was a stunned silence. Then Wang asked, "What were those men doing here so far from their own land?"

"They are fighting a war with the Viet Minh and came here to find me," Farouche said. "They had hoped I would help them. But I refused to join their war because of my other activities. They were very angry with me."

Phong frowned in anger. "I knew you would be much trouble someday, Brother Phap. You do not belong here in the opium mountains."

"I have earned my place," Farouche said angrily. He calmed down and sneered at Wang. "And there are not hundreds of them. Only thirteen."

"Thirteen!" Wang exclaimed. "It could not be."

"Their leader is a war chief called Falconi," Farouche said. "And he has a demon inside him. So do each his men. That is why they can fight so well."

Wang pointed an accusing finger at the Frenchman. "My people said they saw many of your men from Faroucheville with them."

"That is true," Farouche said, unconcerned. "And we fought in the company of those Americans against you." He decided to play on the Meos' superstitions. "Falconi performed many tricks and small miracles. I was much afraid of his power."

"Did they live among you?" Xan asked.

"Yes," Farouche said. Suddenly he noted an opportunity to build up a reputation as a potentially unbeatable enemy. "And they all bedded with women in our village. All of them now carry their men-children."

"Ah!" scoffed Phong. "How do you know this?"

"Our elder wise man told us," Farouche said quickly, adding to the lie. "And he said the unborn will indoubtedly inherit many of the strange powers the fathers possessed."

Genuine fear danced across the features of the other warlords. "What will come of this?" Xan asked.

"The Americans departed as my friends," Farouche

said. "But they must be destroyed or they will come back with more of their brothers to take away our opium."

"How can we kill them? They are invincible devils!" Wang wailed.

"Calm yourself, Brother Wang," Farouche said. "If we get help from the Chinese, the thirteen American devils will be killed. When they do not return to their people, their leaders will be afraid to send more among us. They will think we can counteract their magic."

"The Chinese will not come down here to do this!" Xan shouted in frustration. "I have asked them in the past to visit us in our land."

"That is true," Phong echoed. "They refuse to cross their borders under any circumstances." He looked carefully into the Frenchman's face. "But perhaps you know of a way, Brother Phap."

"No," Farouche said. "But I have learned from the Americans that a strong country in the north of Vietnam are brothers with the Chinese. They have a large army and they will destroy the thirteen Americans if their Chinese brothers ask them to do so."

"Use your radio talking-machine," Phong begged Farouche. "Talk to the Chinese and tell them to have this thing done for us."

Farouche smiled. "Dear Brother Phong, I already have."

The Black Eagles stumbled across the road by chance.

Without proper maps of the local area, all Archie could do was to lead the detachment in a southerly direction while keeping his eyes open for dangerous situations. When he found the primitive highway, he signaled a halt and sent word for Falconi to come forward.

The two of them stood at the edge of the jungle. Archie was exuberant. "Look at them tire tracks, sir! Trucks made 'em, and it looks like there's regular traffic."

Falconi lit a cigarette. "There's some real food for thought here, Archie. If we could get a couple of trucks, we could make a run down this road as far as we could dare go, then hop back into the jungle again."

"Damn, sir!" Archie said. "That'd give us some quick, long-distance traveling. We'd eat up a lot o' ground and it'd sure cut down the time we're out here."

"There's a couple of tricks involved, though," Falconi said. "The first thing is to get the trucks. After that, it'll be touch and go while we roar down a road we know nothing about."

"Fuck it," Archie said. "As long as we're moving south, who cares?"

"Hell, we could drive straight into a division of NVA if we're not careful," Falconi said.

Archie shrugged and spoke in his characteristically simple way. "Then let's be careful."

"But first, let's get some trucks," Falconi said. "Pass the word back to get Swift Elk and Chris up here. We've got an ambush to set up."

Within a quarter of an hour, the detachment had organized itself into its usual ambush formation. Paulo Garcia and Frank Matsamura sealed in the front while Blue Richards and Doc Robichaux prepared to do the same to the rear. The remainder of the detachment, on both sides of the road, was stretched out between them.

The one exception was Archie Dobbs, who was beyond even Blue and Doc. He had a Prick-Six radio with him as he waited for any potential victims to show up.

Two hours after the ambush was organized, Archie got on the horn. "Falcon, this is Scout. A convoy of one-two trucks approaching at about thirty miles per. Over."

"Roger, Scout," Falconi said. "Team Leaders, let this one slip through. Too big. I say again. No action. No action. Confirm. Over."

"Falcon, this is Alpha," Chris responded. "Wilco. Out."

"Falcon, this is Bravo," Swift Elk said over his radio. "Roger that confirmation. Out."

Ten minutes later a dozen North Vietnamese army trucks rolled through the area. The drivers were blissfully unaware that thirteen M16 rifles, manned by one of the toughest anti-Red fighting units in Southeast Asia, were trained on them.

Another hour crawled by without incident.

Then Archie hit the transmit button one more time. "Falcon, this is scout. We got four trucks. Looks like they're moving at about thirty miles per hour. Over."

Falconi felt better about this one. "Roger, Scout. We'll hit these babies. Team leaders confirm. Over."

"Let's go. Out." Chris said.

"Wilco for the Bravos," Swift Elk transmitted.

The caravan of vehicles rolled into the ambush site, past Blue Richards and Doc Robichaux. It continued on through both the Alpha and Bravo teams.

Up front, Paulo Garcia listened for the sounds of the engines. Finally, the first vehicle, a Soviet GAZ-63 two-ton truck, came into his view. The marine set his sights dead on the windshield in front of the driver's face and pumped the trigger.

The glass shattered and the truck turned sharply as the dead driver let the wheel go. It rolled over and burst into flames.

The second truck came to an abrupt halt and the third damned near slammed into its rear. The man in that truck leaped from the cab to scream angry obscenities at the sloppy driving habits of his buddy, but was slammed against his vehicle by a salvo from the guns of Chris Hawkins and Hank Valverde.

The second driver made a stupid move to escape by jumping to the roadway and running toward the jungle. He left the road and scrambled up the embankment where Dwayne Simpson was hidden. The Black Eagles fired one

189

quick shot at close range into the NVA's head. Powder-burned and dead, he rolled back down the dirt roadway.

The fourth man, more experienced, immediately figured out what was going on. He hit his brakes and slammed the gearshift into reverse. But before he could move, Blue Richards and Doc Robichaux riddled the rear of the cab. The man inside was flown forward into the steering wheel by the force of the slugs, and the door flew open allowing his body to tumble out to the dirt highway.

It was over almost as soon as it began.

Swift Elk, ever the intelligence man, went to the burning first truck and managed to reach inside the cab and remove the papers from the glove compartment. The Sioux knew this would be the highest ranking man's vehicle. That meant, as in all Communist armies, he would have the only official documents.

Swift Elk sorted through them until he found what he was looking for. He waved it at Falconi, who was walking toward him.

"Sir, we have a map now."

"That should make Archie's job a hell of a lot easier," Falconi said. He took the chart from Swift Elk and gave it a quick going over. "According to this, we're on People's Highway 51." He grinned in delight. "Hell! There's not an outpost, village, or anything for the next fifty miles."

"That's going to save us a hell of a lot of walking," Swift Elk said.

"And time," Falconi added. "Time—that's our real enemy."

Chief Brewster, meanwhile, had hopped up into the cab of the second truck. He restarted the engine, then moved slowly forward to the burning vehicle in front of him. He carefully bumped against it, then gunned the accelerator and shoved it off the side of the road out of the way.

Archie joined them after looking over both trucks they'd be using. "Them guys must've gassed up recently, sir. The tanks are three-quarters full and there's extra jerry cans o' gas on the sides."

"Here's a present for you," Falconi said. "We figured you could use it."

"A map!" Archie said. He winked at the commander. "Jeez! This takes all the fun out of things." But he was sincerely glad to get the topographic chart.

Falconi didn't want to hang around the area too long. "Okay, guys. Let's move! Command Element in the cab and Alpha Team on the back of the first truck. Bravos, take the second."

Swift Elk signaled to his team. "Double-time! Doc, you drive. I'll ride shotgun. Blue and Dwayne in the back."

The engines were gunned, clutches popped, and the little convoy began the fifty-mile run south.

Sixty miles south of where the ambush had gone down, a radio message was received in a North Vietnamese Motorized Infantry Battalion Headquarters. The transmitted words were quickly copied down. The operator leaped from his chair and rushed from the commo shack across the compound to headquarters.

He stopped in front of the sergeant major's desk. "An important message for the comrade major!"

Without hesitating, the NCO took the paper into his commander's office. "A critical missive, comrade major."

The officer read it, his eyes alight with excitement. He grabbed his helmet, combat gear, and weapon. "Call out the First Company!" he yelled at the sergeant major. "Get them aboard trucks. Full battle load."

"Yes, comrade major," the NCO replied. "Have we been attacked?"

"There isn't time to explain," the major said. "But I'll personally be in command. We are going north on the People's Highway 51 to begin a search for enemy infiltrators."

The sergeant major ran from the headquarters building shrilly blowing on his whistle. Within moments, the well-drilled soldiers had stopped all activity and grabbed their combat gear.

In ten minutes, the motorized rifle company was ready to mount trucks and move out to search of their quarry.

CHAPTER 20

Frank Matsamura took the second shift as air guard in the first truck of the two-vehicle convoy that streaked south on People's Highway Number 51.

This unpleasant task meant that he had to stand up in the back of the truck and keep an eye out for any enemy aircraft—or friendly ones to signal to—and also to stay alert for things in the road ahead. The Japanese-American had to lean against the cab and face into the wind. He eliminated much of the discomfort, however, by wearing his jump goggles and tying his camouflaged neck scarf around his face to protect his nose and mouth from dust, insects, and other miscellaneous flying debris.

The air guard in the second truck was Hank Valverde. He faced to the rear—or "aft," as Chief Brewster would have said—to look out for any interlopers, airborne or groundborne, who might try to sneak up on them. The rest of the men in both trucks kept watch on the right or left sides of the vehicles, depending on which side they were on.

The road they traveled was a crude but relatively smooth because of the dry season. There were a few unavoidable ruts, but for the most part the rustic highway offered possibilities for high speed. It was straight, with only a few slight turns across the flatlands that flowed out from the Meos' home mountains. Both drivers kept their feet down hard on the accelerators to coax as much speed as possible out of the vehicles.

Unfortunately, the Soviet GAZ-63 trucks had been maintained by ill-trained North Vietnamese mechanics, and were capable of only a top speed of thirty miles an hour. Even then, the engines strained and the transmissions groaned with the effort.

Archie Dobbs, in the cab of the first truck with Falconi and Chief Brewster, kept himself up to date on their location with the help of the map that the Chief had pulled from the burning truck. He made careful note of each bend in the road and terrain feature, keeping his finger on the exact spot on the map.

Falconi, in the passenger seat, glanced over at his scout. "How're we doing, Archie?"

"We've made about fifteen miles, sir," Archie answered. "According to this here map, there's no villages or nothing for about another thirty or thirty-five."

Falconi leaned forward to catch the Chief's attention. "Keep your eye on the odometer, Chief. We'll ditch these trucks in another twenty-five miles."

"Aye, aye, sir." The Chief glanced at the instrument panel. "Damn their eyes! The speedometer is in kilometers, so I suppose the odometer is, too."

"Okay, Chief," Falconi said, doing some quick mental figuring. "We'll go another—let's see—uh, forty kilometers, got it?"

"Aye, aye, sir," the Chief replied in his best naval manner. "Forty kilometers."

Archie laughed. "Christ! You'd think you was on a ship, Chief." He pointed to the left. "Keep eyes on the starboard side there."

Chief Brewster scowled. "That's *port*, you lubber."

Archie laughed again and imitated a boatswain's whistle. "Attention all hands! The cap'n wants to see you on the pointy end o' the boat! Pipe the admiral through the porthole and batten down the mate's head!"

Now the Chief laughed. "You dumb shit. Keep your eyes on the chart, okay?"

"Aye, aye," Archie said. He continued his task for another five minutes before he spoke. "Better slow down, Chief. There's some sharp curves coming up pretty quick. From the contour lines on this map I'd say we're moving into some country with plenty of gulleys."

Chief Brewster let up on the accelerator a bit and allowed the straining truck to ease back to twenty-five miles an hour. Frank Matsamura wiped at the dust on his goggles and peered ahead. He could easily see the winding road ahead—and that wasn't all.

"Enemy vehicles!" he yelled, banging on the top of the cab.

The Chief hit the brakes and stopped. Falconi opened the door and stepped out on the running board. "What's happening, Frank?"

"Eight trucks ahead, sir," Frank reported. "And full o' NVA troops—I think." He pulled his binoculars from their case and quickly focused them in. "Oh, yeah! No doubt about it."

Falconi pointed forward. "Chief, drive the truck up to the big embankment where the road takes a sharp turn." He signaled back to Doc Robichaux the other driver. "Pull up beside us."

"I get it," Archie said. "Them NVAs will come roaring around the corner and run straight into these trucks, huh?"

"That's it, Archie," Falconi said. "And we'll be waiting to take advantage of the situation." He leaped to the roadway. "Chris! Swift Elk! Report to me on the double!"

In less than three minutes the trucks were properly arranged and the Black Eagles were in hidden positions on both sides of the road. Archie cranked the charging handle on his M16. "Ambush," he said, "is beginning to be our

195

middle name."

The wait was an ominous one. At first there was silence. Only a few buzzing insects and singing birds sounded over the scene. Then gradually, the sound of whining military truck motors could barely be heard in the distance. The sound grew steadily louder.

"Goddamn!" Archie exclaimed. "There's a lot of 'em."

"Yeah," Falconi beside him agreed. "I would've preferred to let 'em go past us, but there was no place to conceal our vehicles. There would've been a fight in any case, and I prefer for it to begin to our advantage."

"Yeah," Archie agreed. "Good thinking, sir."

Now the motors were a roar in the ears of the Black Eagles. But suddenly there was a squeal of poorly maintained brakes followed by a sickening collision of metal. Cries of fear and pain sounded as more of the trucks piled into the first, until the chain-reaction crash had involved all eight vehicles in the convoy.

"Fire!" Falconi yelled.

Thirteen M16s kicked loose and pounded bullets into the crowd of troops grouped together in the backs of the trucks. The effect was devastating as whole groups of NVA slumped against each other in the press of flying slugs.

But this North Vietnamese unit was made up of veterans who had returned from the south after hard campaigning against the Americans and their ARVN comrades-in-arms. The surviving squad leaders quickly organized the unwounded. Very quickly, the NVA began to return fire. At the same time they withdrew from the exposed area and moved into the jungle.

"Damn!" Chief Brewster said in admiration. "Those swabs are damned good!"

"Too good," Falconi said. He noted the area was now empty of combat effectives. He yelled out, "Cease fire!"

The cessation of shooting left a void of silence over the scene. Once more there were no sounds, not even from the wounded, and it seemed they were in a vacuum.

Out in the Alpha Team, the farthest forward, Frank Matsamura's eyes danced back and forth as he scanned the heavy brush ahead for a sighting of the enemy.

There was nothing.

Farther back, Dwayne Simpson with his buddies in the Bravos also tried to figure out what the hell was going down in the weird situation.

Stillness and silence.

Archie slowly crawled backward from his fighting position until he joined up with Falconi. "I don't like this shit," he whispered.

"Me neither," Falconi softly agreed. "We're going to break contact." He pressed the transmit button on the Prick-Six. "Team Leaders, this is Falcon. Move to the rear. Slow and easy. Out."

Chief Brewster was actually the man closest to the crashed trucks. He'd bobbed his head up and down to see if there were any brave infiltrators trying to work their way through the wreckage toward them. He could see nothing. The navy seal listened intently, then slowly stood up and tried to peer over a pile of NVA bodies.

The shot exploded from the jungle across the road.

The round hit Chief P.O. Leland Brewster under the left eye, popping it out. His head jerked back under the impact and he fell straight back into the bushes—dead before his body hit the soft ground.

An eruption of bellowing voices punctuated by full-automatic fire from AK47s followed and a mass attack rolled out of the trees and crossed the road into the jungle where the Black Eagles were positioned.

The Command Element and the Alpha Team caught the brunt of the assault. They were barely able to pump off a few rounds into the khaki-clad mob of NVA before having to turn tail and run like hell deeper into the monsoon forest.

Swift Elk, a bit farther away with his men, was able to direct only a smattering of covering fire before the Bravos, too, were running like hell with what seemed the entire North Vietnamese Army on their asses.

The Black Eagles tried to keep some semblance of unit integrity, but it was almost impossible. The best Falconi could hope for was that they could break the close contact long enough to set up some sort of firing position to begin a more orderly rear-guard type of retreat.

Individual efforts were the unissued orders of the day.

Swift Elk discovered a perfect tree with a low fork in it. He circled around it and swung the muzzle of his rifle toward the enemy. On full-auto he rocked-and-rolled 5.56 millimeter slugs into the crowd surging toward him. He slowed them down, but others continued to press forward.

After one more burst, the Sioux Indian was forced to flee once again.

Down on the far side of the Black Eagle line, Dwayne Simpson could do little but run with all the speed he could muster. He flashed across bushes and leaped fallen trees as bullets smacked and whined around him. At one point he leaped around in a whirling motion to send a wild, un-aimed spray of bullets at his pursuers. Then, luckily, he crashed into the good cover offered by a stand of bamboo. Cutting diagonally toward the center like a wide receiver going for the bomb in the NFL, he outdistanced the NVA troops enough to lessen the danger he was in.

Frank Matsamura also leaped into that same bamboo grove, but he was three dozen yards from the point where Dwayne had found cover. Here the springy green and yellow stalks were thick and heavy. Frank became quickly entangled and was forced to kick and swing his rifle to get free. But it didn't work.

Six NVA crashed in behind him and a half-dozen Kalashnikov assault rifle muzzles spurted flame and 7.62 millimeter lead into the brave Japanese-American.

198

Frank went down with ten slugs in him. His body didn't cease functioning immediately. Years of self-discipline and meditation in the martial arts came to his stead. He rolled over and came up with his trigger finger squeezing two bursts of full-automatic to dump four of his attackers to the ground.

Then blood came up into Frank's mouth and he managed to fire again as he died a samurai's death.

Hank Valverde had been slightly ahead of Frank and was able to keep moving. He found himself suddenly in thick brush, and he took advantage by diving straight to the ground. Whirling around in the dirt, he began shooting from the prone position. Unseen by the enemy, he did them terrible damage. Then, with the pressure again building up, he backed out of the position and turned to continue his flight.

An hour later the battle was over.

No one was sure how it ended. The NVA had done their damnedest, but even a hundred men could do little to a dozen others who could eventually fight back in an effective manner as they penetrated deeper and deeper into the primitive, heavily overgrown jungle countryside.

Now, exhausted and stunned, the Black Eagles licked their wounds. Two men were missing and presumed dead. But the survivors still had plenty of ammunition and determination.

Archie Dobbs had little to say, for a change. He hung his head in stunned silence. "Damn! There must've been a million of them bastards!"

Falconi was more realistic. "I'd estimate that we were hit by a reinforced motorized rifle company."

"It don't matter if it was them or the King's Grenadier Guards," Archie said. "We got two dead guys back there."

Falconi sighed. "Like most of our KIAs, we'll have to leave 'em."

Archie had a bad habit of dwelling on unpleasant

subjects. "I don't suppose we've brung back more'n a half dozen out of the guys we've lost, huh?"

"We have more to worry about than that now!" Falconi snapped.

"Yes, sir," Archie agreed. "We got to get the hell outta this area."

"You have the map," Falconi said. "Go to it, Tiger."

Archie had spent ten minutes orienting himself with the chart from the glove compartment. He looked up at his commanding officer. "I know where we are now, sir."

"Good," Falconi answered. "And we only have one way to go. Back to the north to get the hell away from this district."

Swift Elk took a drink from his canteen. "That's back to Farouche's country, sir."

"It can't be helped," Falconi said. "We've got to start over."

Archie didn't need any particular orders. He stood up, adjusted his gear, and signaled to the others. "Let's go, Black Eagles. *Calcitra clunis!*"

The men got to their feet, formed up in teams, and moved off to whatever adventure the fickle Goddess of War had in store for them next.

The Black Eagles spent the remainder of the day moving fast but silently through the thick vegetation. They had been forced to stop on numerous occasions by the proximity of the NVA troops who were combing the jungle for them. But the search was ill organized and haphazard, pushed by the haste of the Red commander.

Toward evening, Archie was beginning to feel more confident. He picked up the pace a bit, but still maintained a personal state of extreme alertness.

Then he was forced to come to a halt.

The noise that had disturbed him continued to grow

louder. The scout carefully situated himself behind a bamboo tree. Using the drooping leaves as cover, he peered outward. Finally he found what was creating the disturbance. Red-turbaned Meos, obviously searching and reconnoitering, moved through the brush.

Archie brought up his Prick-Six radio and spoke softly into the mouthpiece. "Falcon. This is Scout. We've just run into Farouche. I'll be coming back to join you. Out." Slowly, cautiously, Archie retraced his steps to rejoin the detachment that now waited for him.

The Black Eagles were virtually right back where they had started.

CHAPTER 21

Lt. Col. Robert Falconi had neither the time nor the inclination for any high-toned tactical maneuvers.

His quickly conceived plan of battle was to pull back far enough from Lucien Farouche and his Meos to avoid contact, yet not to such a great distance as to bump into the NVA unit still searching for them. The next step would be to circle around the Frenchman, then pile into the rear of his unit with M16s blazing.

With both Chief Brewster and Frank Matsamura gone, the overall strength of the Black Eagles had gone from thirteen to eleven.

Archie, as usual, led the way. He made sure the detachment skirted the Meos at a safe distance as they moved through the jungle doing the silent Georgia high-step to avoid making unnecessary noises such as cracking dried twigs or kicking rocks around.

It took almost two hours for the painstaking maneuver, but in the end it was worth it. Strung out in a skirmish line, Falconi and his men didn't have much depth in their attack, but they had balls and enough desperation to hit hard.

They stepped off slowly, gradually increasing their speed until they were practically trotting when they crashed into the back of Farouche's small army. Hank Valverde and

Dwayne Simpson took advantage of their rifles' M203 launchers, which would throw 40-millimeter grenades four hundred meters.

The firing of grenades was coordinated with full-automatic sweeps from the weapons of Paulo Garcia and Blue Richards. The detonations and overlapping streams of 175 rounds per minute of 5.56 millimeter slugs blew the nearest groups of Meos away like chaffs of straw in the wind.

The Black Eagles advanced over the bodies of their victims, their disciplined fire punching into the confused, milling tribesmen who had once been their comrades-in-arms.

Farther forward, in the vanguard of his primitive troops, Lucien Farouche turned to look back at the disturbance. He could not see the damage being done to his force, but within moments Ming appeared from the scene of fighting.

"Commandant! Commandant!" the Meo yelled. "It is monsieur le colonel and his men!"

"What in *le nom du Dieu* are those bastards doing back there?" Farouche demanded. "I thought they would be traveling almost directly in a southerly course."

"They have hit us from the rear," Ming explained breathlessly. "Many of our men have died."

"I must gain control of the situation," Farouche said. He then bellowed his orders loud enough so that they could be heard throughout the vicinity of the battle. "*Tournez—* turn! The bastards are behind us!"

The Meos farther forward had been confused and unsettled by the noise of the fighting. They had expected nc action there, and the unexpected combat caused them a great deal of bewilderment. Being more primitive warriors than trained modern soldiers, they had simply milled around while their bretheren were being butchered behind them.

But Farouche's shouted orders got them moving.

Chris Hawkins, acting as a rifleman, and Doc Robichaux beside him were beginning to think they and their buddies were going to march straight through the jungle to an easy victory. Hank Valverde and Dwayne Simpson kept grenades detonating ahead of them with comforting regularity; Paulo and Blue were carrying on like they were walking machine gun nests; and Falconi, Archie, and Swift Elk were coming on like the Three Musketeers.

The Meo dead were piling up in front of the detachment like slaughtered goats. At that particular time, the only trouble Falconi's men were experiencing was having to stumble and leap over the enemy dead.

Then the wall of enemy *living* burst through the trees and stormed toward them. The Black Eagles advance came to a stop.

Hank and Dwayne did their best to step up their rate of fire, but the Meos were closing in so fast that the intrepid grenadiers were soon shooting with their launching tubes level instead of elevated.

Falconi went from semi- to full-automatic to add a bit more fire power to Paulo and Blue's efforts. The remaining three guys on semi-fire stepped up their rate of trigger pulls, but Farouche's force pressed on stubbornly and stupidly into the steel hail being thrown up at them.

"Move back!" Falconi finally ordered. "Slow! Slow! Keep up your rate of fire or those sons of bitches are going to be down our throats!"

The tribesmen, shrieking hideously in their battle rage, pushed and pulled their dead and wounded away as they pressed forward.

The Black Eagles now deliberately stepped rearward in a measured pace as they used sheer naked firepower to hold off a numerically superior enemy. Finally, they stumbled back into a heavily overgrown depression.

"Hold here!" Falconi ordered. He positioned the grenadiers and automatic riflemen across the small space. "All M16s, full auto!"

The fusillade doubled in intensity, the sheer force finally stopping the attack. Gradually, like they hated doing it, the Meos moved away from the fiery hell they faced.

Then contact was broken altogether.

Silence reigned over the battle site. The only sounds were fresh magazines being slapped into receivers as the Black Eagles took advantage of the lull.

"How's the ammo!" Hank Valverde asked around. As supply sergeant, that was his worry.

"Hell," Archie said summing up everyone's situation. "I'm loaded down with the stuff. I could start a civil war of my own."

"At least that's a change to what we generally face," Swift Elk said. "We can last one hell of a long time here."

"Yeah," Falconi agreed. "There's only one thing that can whip us—numbers."

"There's plenty of 'em all right," Archie remarked.

An outbreak of yells and screams sounded out in the jungle, punctuated by the sound of running sandaled feet rapidly approaching.

"Shit," Dwayne Simpson said, raising his grenade launcher, "and here come the motherfuckers!"

CHAPTER 22

Once more the jungle glen exploded with gunshots and detonating grenades. The Meos, though suffering horribly, slowly closed in until the combatants could make out each other's facial features in the whirling hell of the fighting.

Finally, Lucien Farouche could be seen directing his men. The Frenchman's hatred for the Americans who had destroyed his hopes of dominating the northern Laotian opium trade was feeding fuel to his enflamed Gallic temper.

"En avant, bâtards!" he screamed and cursed at his men. "Kill the *merdes!* Destroy them!"

The Meos, caring only to fight now, became more reckless. Their battle lust drove them on, yet this fierce bravery could not penetrate the horrible firepower being poured into them by Falconi and his Black Eagles.

This inability to annihilate the Americans frustrated and infuriated Farouche until his frail sanity, threadbare after fifteen years in the wilds, finally snapped.

He didn't care about his own life anymore. The ember of hatred he'd had for Falconi had been growing steadily, until it burst into flame and consumed what remnants of sanity he had.

In his twisted mind he was no longer the chief of opium-smuggling Meos. He was once again Sgt. Lucien Farouche of the colonial paras, sporting the red beret and leopard-style camouflage uniform of his old battalion. There were no Black Eagles to consider in his mental processes either; only Viet Minh concealed in the jungle grove ahead.

Yet his thoughts could still picture a man he hated with all his soul and being—Monsieur le Colonel Robert Falconi.

"Cher Saint Michel, aidez-moi!" he bellowed, praying to the patron saint of paras. Holding on to a Chinese 7.62 millimeter automatic pistol, he pushed his way through the crowd of struggling Meos until he was in front of them.

The Black Eagles who spotted the Frenchman instinctively lifted their fire. His bizarre appearance fascinated them in a gruesome sort of way, and they subconsciously all wanted to see what the crazy bastard was going to do.

Farouche raced across the space between his front lines and the Black Eagle positions. He leaped over a startled Archie Dobbs who had assumed a prone position in the center of the line, and charged into the interior.

"Falconi!" Farouche screamed, firing his pistol wildly in the air. "Falconi!"

Falconi, squatting behind in the cover provided by a large *rung ram* tree, stood up. At the exact moment Farouche stumbled past, the American stepped out and grabbed the arm holding the Chinese handgun. A quick pull of Falconi caused Farouche to stumble. A *shuto* punch to the forearm made the Frenchman drop his weapon with a bellow of rage and pain.

"Hello, commandant," Falconi said with a smile.

Farouche snarled and leaped at Falconi's throat. The Black Eagles commander took one step back, then made a double-handed *haishu* outward punch that broke the grip around his neck.

The Frenchman again yelled in pain, but, as it might a charging bull, the discomfort seemed to give him energy. He leaped forward to attack again, but Falconi was waiting. He pivoted on his left foot and delivered a lightning-quick *sokuto* kick with the right.

Farouche's head snapped back and his neck broke.

Blood immediately seeped from his eyes, nose, and ears as he turned and staggered back toward his men. The Meos stared incredulously at their master, who now weaved weakly.

"Commandant! Commandant!"

Ming emerged from the combat formation and hurried toward Farouche. But he was too late. The former colonial parachutist pitched forward on his face.

Dwayne Simpson, never one to let an opportunity to create a dramatic scene pass by, aimed his grenade launcher downward and pulled the trigger.

The explosion went off between Farouche's corpse and Ming, sending hunks of both men whirling through the air.

Then the Black Eagles braced themselves for the final attack. But the Meos made no threatening motions until, finally, they moved back. Slowly, in groups of six and seven, the tribesmen abandoned the battlefield, completely demoralized.

But the detachment's relief was short-lived.

Khaki uniforms suddenly appeared among the withdrawing Meos and moved forward toward the Black Eagles position.

The NVA motorized rifle company had caught up with them.

The Red infantrymen were as surprised to find the Americans as Falconi and his men were to see them suddenly show up. The North Vietnamese commander barked a few terse orders that sent his well-drilled veteran troops into a quick enveloping maneuver.

The attack, quickly ordered and virtually unorganized, was easily beaten back with disciplined fire. The battle broke off and the Black Eagles took advantage of the lull to hastily dig fighting holes to reinforce their position.

Archie Dobbs, being a member of neither fire team, was able to leave the perimeter and move deeper into the stand of jungle brush. He took a quick recon of the place, then rushed excitedly back to Falconi. "Sir!"

The colonel turned from his duties. "Yeah, Archie?"

"There's a little spring deeper into the brush there," Archie reported. "The water is clear and cool."

"That's a break," Falconi said. "It looks like we might have to stay here for quite a while."

Archie shrugged to show his lack of worry. "What the hell, colonel? We got plenty of rations and ammo. With that water, and in this cover, we can hold off an army."

"Maybe not an army," Falconi disagreed. "But we can sure as hell give that company of motorized infantry a run for their goddamned money!" He pointed forward. "Join the Alphas as a rifleman, Archie. With Frank Matsamura gone, they're short a man."

"Yes, sir."

Falconi situated himself in the center of the position to direct things. After a brief commo check with both fire teams, he relaxed and waited.

An eerie silence had settled over the jungle. With the animals and insects driven away by the battle, there was no sound whatsoever for almost an hour. Then a steady whacking of machetes and digging spades could be heard coming from where the NVA had evidently set themselves up.

Ray Swift Elk, his canteen now full of the fresh spring water, treated himself to a cool drink. "What the hell's going on out there?" he asked Blue Richards next to him. "Are those bastards digging in?"

Blue grinned. "Maybe they're expecting *us* to attack *them*, huh?"

Swift Elk screwed the cap shut on the canteen. "Who knows?"

A half hour more of the activity followed, then there was

silence once more.

Falconi raised his head as some instinct caused a shot of nervous tension to shoot through his body. Then he heard the sounds.

Whump! Whump! Whump! Whump!

Suddenly he realized what it was. Mortar shells were being dropped down tubes. "Hit the dirt!" he yelled. "Incoming rounds!"

The first explosions were off a bit, but pretty soon the barrage begun to creep slowly toward the Black Eagles. It was only a matter of minutes before they'd blown to hell—blasted into atoms—in this final battle.

CHAPTER 23

The detonating mortar shells were now so close that the concussion of the explosions rocked the trees and blew dust across the position.

"Move in on me! On the double!" Falconi yelled.

Ray Swift Elk leaped up, grabbing Blue Richards by the collar. He hauled the navy seal to his feet and shouted to Dwayne Simpson and Doc Robichaux, "Head for the center of the position! Let's go!"

The Bravo Team crashed through the dense vegetation to join their commanding officer.

Chris Hawkins, alerting his Alphas, waited for Paulo Garcia, Hank Valverde, and Archie Dobbs to pull out before he followed. A mortar round crashed nearby, forcing the navy officer to dive to cover.

After waiting a bit, he leaped to his feet to follow his team when another shell landed at the direct edge of the perimeter. The fuse, with a striker device, blew off the charge when it struck the ground. Pieces and hunks of shrapnel flared out on all sides.

Chris went down, his back lacerated by the metal chunks. His face hit the dirt, and when he raised it he was amazed that he did not see a stand of jungle brush and trees.

Instead, he eyes beheld a rocky New England beach.

Chris gazed incredulously at the sight of several old school chums beckoning him to join them at the clam bake they were having. It all seemed rather natural, in a strange, dreamy sort of way. Chris raised a bloody hand to wave and smile at them.

That was the way he died.

There was nothing his Black Eagles buddies could do. Blue Richards, a navy man like the dead officer, hesitated. "I don't know where you're goin', Mister Hawkins," Blue said. "But I hope it's all smooth sailin' and calm seas." He turned away to get back to the business at hand.

"Those mortar rounds are gonna tear this place to hell in about another minute," Falconi said. He was interrupted by another crash of several explosions. The noise had punished their eardrums and he had to shout as he continued explaining what he wanted to do. "Our only chance is to break for the open and run like hell. I don't know what's going to happen, but—"

"What the fuck?" Archie exclaimed, pointing past the colonel.

Falconi whirled around and saw several of Farouche's Meos, wearing their familiar turbans, standing behind him. He, like the others, raised his M16.

But Doc Robichaux leaped out between the tribesmen and the detachment. "Hold your fire!" he yelled. "I know one of 'em!"

The Meo stepped forward. "You saved my son's life, monsieur le docteur. Now I and my kinsmen will repay this debt to you in a fitting manner."

"How the hell did you get in here?" Falconi demanded.

"There is an overgrown hidden valley leading out of this grove," the Meo explained. "In here is located a tunnel of vegetation leading to it."

Suddenly Falconi remembered. "Sari mentioned a place like this. But she didn't know the location."

"This is it," the Meo said. "These vines and brush are so

212

thick that one can walk upon them. Many years ago, our people constructed this secret passage for the opium trade. It is how we came here with the commandant to seek you."

"Sari told me this tunnel will take us to a valley that opens on a safe route to the south," Falconi said. "How far does it go?"

The Meo shrugged. "I know nothing of distances. But I can tell you this: You will find safety from this place. You kept us from an easy retreat when you blundered in here. The rest of our people went past the Viet Minh soldiers. I, and the men of my family, came back through the tunnel."

A half-dozen mortar shells now landed directly on the edge of the perimeter. The NVA gunners had now found the range. It would only be moments before the final killing barrage would crash down on them.

"Let's get the hell out of here!" Falconi yelled over the noise.

The Meos turned and seemed to be walking out into the open. But they ducked and crawled under a stand of *rung* bushes. Archie, pushed forward by Falconi, went directly after them. At first he thought he was going into thick brush, but he finally realized he was crawling through a tunneled-out section of jungle bushes. He glanced back to make sure the others were following, then went on quickly, following the tribesmen.

This man-made cave was not quite a hundred meters long. It opened onto a deep gash in the earth's surface that led down into a wide valley. The Meos stopped and waited for the Black Eagles to emerge into the opening.

Doc's friend pointed in the direction of the open country. "If you go that way, you will find a good trail south. We opium smugglers have used it for many, many years. You can avoid villages and soldiers, but you must live off the jungle."

"That we can do," Falconi said.

Doc Robichaux came up and offered his hand. "Many

213

thanks, friend."

"My son would be dead if it weren't for you," the Meo said. "And you must never forget that he has part of your soul. You breathed it into him."

Falconi was puzzled. "What the hell does he mean by that?"

"Mouth-to-mouth resuscitation," Doc explained. He turned to the Meo. "Your son and I will meet in the afterlife."

The Meo put a hand on Doc's shoulder. "You are my brother."

Doc smiled and answered in kind. "You are my brother."

Archie was impatient. "Enough of this shit! Let's haul ass the hell outta here. We still got a long walk back to South Vietnam."

"Lead on, scout," Falconi said. He turned to Paulo Garcia and Hank Valverde. "Fall in the middle of the column. The Alpha Team is finished for a while."

"We'll be ready for the next mission, sir," Paulo said. "C'mon, Hank. Let's give them Bravos some backing up."

The Black Eagles detachment formed a single column and moved out toward the valley that stretched before them.

The Meos stood silently and watched the Americans depart from their country. Then they turned and headed north back to Faroucheville.

The opium trade was still alive and kicking.

CHAPTER 24

Lt. Col. Robert Falconi walked to the edge of Camp Nui Dep's chopper pad and turned to watch the H34 lift off. The aircraft made a lazy half-circle to the south then headed back toward its home base.

The other Black Eagles, the surviving eight, waited for their commanding officer to come off the landing area. When he walked by, they dutifully fell into formation behind him and followed him back through the camp to their bunker.

The other troops in the camp, Maj. Rory Riley's Special Forces men, stopped their activities to nod silent greetings at the men newly returned from combat. The Green Berets didn't know where Falconi's men had been or what they had done, but it was obvious that some big operation had been brought to a conclusion.

The Black Eagles had walked through jungle for two weeks. They had lived off the land, while the wiley Archie Dobbs had guided them toward friendly territory. They finally reached an ARVN ranger outpost with American advisors. After they made radio contact with SOG headquarters in Saigon, a helicopter had been immediately dispatched for them.

Now the camp commander Maj. Rory Riley stood by his

own bunker as the detachment walked by. He instinctively counted them, noting silently that three of the original were not present.

"Nice to see you guys," he said.

There were a few waves and slight smiles, but no spoken words. Now that the ordeal was over, the exhaustion was beginning to set in. Muscles were tightening and fatigue pushed the remaining energy away from hard-used bodies.

When Falconi's men reached their earthen billets, they found Chuck Fagin waiting for them. He had already been advised of the KIAs via radio, and he knew the men were in no mood for stupid jokes. He had planned a surprise for them and was going to make a big deal out of it, but he had second thoughts. He just told them what he'd done.

"I got you guys a refrigerator," he said. "There's beer in it."

"Thanks, Fagin," Archie said.

Falconi shifted his combat load on his shoulder. "Ready for a debriefing?"

"Let it wait," the CIA operative said.

The lovesick Archie had more on his mind. "How about our mail?"

"I put it on your bunks," Fagin answered.

They filed down into the bunker, each man stopping at the fridge and grabbing a couple of cold Budweisers. They went to their bunks and deposited their gear.

Archie had one letter and he recognized Betty Lou's handwriting. Excited, he tore it open and began to read:

Dear Archie,
    You'll never know how it pains me to tell you this but it's best that I let you know straight off. I've found someone else, sweet Archie. . . .

He continued reading in stunned silence, then wadded up the letter and tossed it on the bunker floor.

Ray Swift Elk noticed him. "Hey, Arch. Is ever'thing okay?"

Archie took a long drink of the cold suds. "No, goddamnit! Ever'thing ain't okay." He tipped his head back and chug-a-lugged the entire can. When he finished, he threw it angrily against the wall.

"I just got a fucking 'Dear John'!"

"From the nurse?" Hank asked.

Archie sneered. "Who else'd send me one, shithead?"

Blue Richards, unlacing his boots, glanced up into Archie's face. From the expression on the scout's features, Blue knew that particular situation was far from over. "Hey, Arch," Blue said. "Let's have a beer and a sit-down together. We could go out and—"

Archie Dobbs didn't answer. Instead he abruptly left the billets and walked up the steps out of the bunker into the hot afternoon sun slamming down on Nui Dep.

Doc Robichaux popped his second can of beer. "Imagine going without pussy only to get a 'Dear John' from the bitch."

Swift Elk was worried. "I'll tell you guys something," he said. "This is just the beginning of that particular problem. Archie might go slightly insane over this."

The others thought about it for a moment, then turned their attention back to the enjoying one of the best parts of soldiering:

Finally getting in from the field.

EPILOGUE

The Satellite Communications Control Station situated outside of San Diego, California hummed along in its quiet, low-keyed routine.

Deep inside the complex, in one of the monitoring stations, the control consoles in front of the engineers manning them gave every indication that the orbiting spheres of electronic communications equipment were operating as designed as they circled the globe.

One of the technicians, assigned to a specific project designated by acronym SCARS—Special Communication and Reporting Satellite—lazily sipped coffee and watched the screen continue to display its comforting pattern of uninterrupted impulses across its green expanse.

Then it stopped.

The man, unconcerned, reached out with his free hand and gently tapped the RESET key.

Nothing happened.

He tried again. "Oh, hell!" he swore softly. He attempted to reset several more times without success. Finally, exasperated, he did a mini-boot, but still could get no results. Now pissed off, he brought the system down and took it through the complicated steps of a full boot.

Still with nil results.

"Charlie!"

The senior engineer came over and was appraised of the situation. "Goddamnit. You know SCARS isn't supposed to be out of monitor for more than five minutes."

"It won't take a boot," the technician complained.

The senior engineer, pressed a bit for time, tried a mini-boot also, but it wouldn't take. Rather than expend valuable more minutes, he went to systems control and tried a full boot from the computer programming unit.

There were absolutely no positive results.

"Harry!"

The chief engineer was brought onto the scene. He went to the back of the CPU and opened it up to expose the emergency system backup. He went through his assigned alternative routine with no success. Now sweating out a good ass-chewing, since SCARS was now unmonitored for nine minutes, the chief went into full emergency procedures. This involved going into the center's vault and performing an electronic operation that some thought would bring dead men back to life.

But SCARS' screen remained blank.

The senior engineer looked up when the chief engineer came back from the vault. "Now what do we do?"

"There's only one guy to call," the chief said.

The senior nodded. "Yeah. Erickson."

"That's the guy that designed this baby," the technician said. He knew things were serious by then. "Where do you find him?"

The senior engineer shrugged. "Start with a call to his plush Pacific Beach apartment."

But the chief engineer shook his head. "If you want to find Erickson, you go where there's flashy women, fast horses, and high-stakes wagering." He walked back to use the phone in his office. "This may take a while."

Frantic calls were made that ranged over the western half of the United States from Del Mar, Santa Anita, Reno, and Las Vegas. After an hour, the chief emerged. "Finally located that highroller. They've sent a company plane for him."

"Great," the senior said. He turned and nudged the technician. "In the meantime, take this baby through every emergency activating procedure in the book."

A feverish three hours followed. Finally, after the tenth repeat of the complicated procedure, an interior phone lit up. The chief, his shirtsleeves rolled up and his necktie undone, quickly grabbed the instrument. "Yeah? All right! Send him up here. What? I don't give a damn if he's got a beautiful dame with him or not! Badge the broad and let her in with him."

The senior wiped at the sweat on his brow. "Erickson?"

"Right." There was no denying the relief in his voice. "He'll put things right."

The door to the room opened ten minutes late and a slim blond man stepped in. A leggy, large-breasted beautiful woman hung on to his arm.

The chief nodded to him. "Hi ya, Erickson."

"What's the trouble, then?"

"SCARS is down and won't respond to booting," the senior said. "You designed this baby, so we figure you're the one to put things right."

Erickson turned and winked at the woman. "This won't take long." He pushed the technician aside and took the man's chair. He began a long series of coding, using programming that he had developed using his design-engineering talents. After twenty minutes he knew what was wrong.

"There's interference that's knocked SCARS out," Erickson said. Then he added ominously, "Man-made interference."

The engineers mouths stood open. Finally the chief spoke. "But, who?"

Erickson stood up. "According to my readings, the jamming is coming from Southeast Asia." He walked to the

221

woman and turned. "North Vietnam, to be exact."

His female companion cooed at him. "Oh, Genie-kins! You're the greatest!"

"Wait a minute, Erickson!" the chief engineer shouted. "You can't leave us like this!"

Erickson shrugged. "Sorry. There's nothing I can do from here. In fact, there's nothing anyone can do from any distance. That sort of purposeful reception counteraction has to be dealt with at the source."

"You mean someone has to go to North Vietnam to end the problem?"

"Exactly," Erickson said. He turned to the woman and winked. "C'mon, baby. Have I ever taken you to the Denny's by the racetrack?"

"Oooh, Genie-kins!" she cooed. "Could we go in your newer car this time?"

The chief engineer watched Erickson leave, then glanced over at the senior engineer. "Where are they going to find any bastards crazy enough to take on a dangerous job like that?"

ACTION ADVENTURE